Morning Star

Morning Star

Judith Plaxton

Second Story Press

Library and Archives Canada Cataloguing in Publication

Plaxton, Judith, 1940-
Morning star / by Judith Plaxton.

ISBN 978-1-897187-97-5

1. Underground Railroad—Juvenile fiction. I. Title.

PS8631.L42M67 2011   jC813'.6   C2011-904503-6

Cover by Luc Normandin

Edited by Alison Kooistra
Copyedited by Kathryn White
Designed by Melissa Kaita
Icons © iStockphoto

Printed and bound in Canada

*Second Story Press gratefully acknowledges the support of the
Ontario Arts Council and the Canada Council for the Arts for our
publishing program. We acknowledge the financial support of the
Government of Canada through the Canada Book Fund.*

 ONTARIO ARTS COUNCIL
CONSEIL DES ARTS DE L'ONTARIO

 Canada Council   Conseil des Arts
for the Arts   du Canada

Published by
Second Story Press
20 Maud Street, Suite 401
Toronto, ON
M5V 2M5
www.secondstorypress.ca

For Lewis, Emmett, Hannah, and Christoph

CHAPTER 1
Flower

FLOWER FELT fingers press down on her mouth, gentle but firm. She struggled awake to see her mother lift them away, touch one against her own lips, eyes wide with silent warning. Cleo helped Flower to sit up, shoved sleepy feet into shoes, and wrapped a cloak around her daughter's shoulders. Gabriel lay on their cot, still asleep, his pudgy mouth open. Lizzie, whom Flower called Aunty, made her silent way toward the family and embraced them one by one.

"What…?" Flower began.

Her expression fierce, Cleo raised a finger once more. Flower stayed quiet, felt her body jerk as her father's strong hands adjusted a sack on her back. She shivered in the chill air and felt rising alarm as she looked at the solemn faces of her mother and Aunty. The two women embraced once more; then Aunty clasped Flower's face in her hands and kissed both cheeks. After the baby was bundled and secured in a sling for Cleo to carry, Eldon returned to the doorway. He looked in both directions and then gestured for his

1

family to come with him out into the dark night.

Flower followed dutifully but reluctantly, still sleepy and confused. They crept out of the bunkhouse and passed by the back kitchen and laundry, the places where Cleo toiled daily preparing food and scrubbing linens, with Flower as her nimble helper. Once outside, Flower tugged at her mother's sleeve. They both stopped. Cleo bent down and whispered directly into her daughter's ear. "Your Pa's taking us away from this place. It's going to be a long road. You must be brave and strong, and quiet as a cat." Cleo straightened and they resumed walking.

There was no moon, and clouds obscured the stars. Flower trailed behind her father. His long strides began to separate them, taking him farther and farther ahead. She quickened her pace, caught her toe on a tree root, and fell to the ground, her mother stumbling into her. Eldon gave his daughter a shake as he helped her up and said softly, "Stay close to me and pick up your feet."

They walked through fields, stalks brushing against them, wet grass soaking the skirts of Cleo and Flower, their hems becoming heavy with dirt. When they arrived at the brook, they removed their shoes and waded into the flowing water. This was where Flower sometimes lingered on a hot day, but it was unfamiliar and scary in the inky blackness. Her feet became numb and slid around on the stones. She was afraid she might trip again, but didn't want to use her voice to ask for help. After a few minutes, her father lifted her out of the cold water and carried her until they reached a bridge. They sat on the bank beneath it and rested.

Twelve-year-old Flower slept briefly, her head in her mother's lap. When it was time to continue, she stood again, shaky with sleep, and walked between her parents. After a while, the dark night evolved into a gray dimness.

"Morning's coming—people might see us! Hurry!"

Eldon's whispered warning was like an alarm. They started to run. Eldon tugged his daughter along, leading the way into a woodlot. As they advanced, it became a forest, the trees tall and protective, like guardians.

They resumed their endless walking. When Flower started to whimper, her mother didn't chastise her. Flower decided her mother probably felt like whimpering too, especially with Gabriel struggling and kicking on her back. Suddenly her father stopped and began to walk in a zigzag fashion—back and forth, side to side, frantically look- ing—for what? He stopped and shook his head, weary and impatient.

"What are you looking for?" her mother asked.

"Four large pines, two smaller ones in front. Due west. I'm going to climb up so I can see farther." He scrambled up a tree, finally standing on a large limb. "There they are, a mile or so up ahead." He stepped down, branch by branch, and jumped to the ground.

It took almost another hour of walking to reach the pine grove. Flower's father stood and scanned the trees, uncertain. Gabriel started to scream and pull at his mother's hair. The sudden onset of his wailing was shocking in the still morning air. Cleo's "shushing" was fierce.

Flower reached up and stroked her brother's face, trying to calm him and keep him quiet. "There, there, Gabriel." She bent her finger into his mouth, and he sucked on her knuckle, his crying reduced to a softer mewling.

Cleo jiggled the baby on her back. "Isn't this far enough?" she asked. "People might hear him if he starts up again. He's beyond hungry. Can't we stop now so I can feed him?"

"Now…a mighty oak." Eldon lifted his hand, asking for patience. Flower studied his face and felt immense relief to see his eyes brighten and his frown disappear.

"There it is!" They threaded their way past the pines and stood in front of a large, mature oak. Eldon scanned the branches and then pointed. Almost out of sight, in the crook of three limbs, a wooden spoon lay laced with twine.

"Twenty paces north." He began to stride, counting his steps. Cleo and Flower followed. They arrived at a rock face, high as the trees, green with clumps of moss. Eldon counted again and stood before a large bush. He pulled the branches aside to reveal a small cave.

They settled inside. There was room for all four of them

to lie down, but not before Cleo pulled bread and fruit from the sack Flower carried. Eldon had drawn water from the brook and had stored it in a small crock. It was still cold and delicious. Cleo nursed Gabriel, and he fell asleep. They had their meal, huddled together, and slept.

CHAPTER 2
Felicia

FELICIA STOOD in front of her bed and contemplated the clothing spread out on it. She picked up a blue sweater, held it to her chest, and turned to the mirror. Her reflection stared back at her, nose scrunched in disgust.

A light rapping of knuckles at the bedroom door. "Felicia!"

"Yes."

Delia's head appeared between the open door and the frame. "It's time to get a move on. Come down and have some breakfast. I've already made it for you."

"Okay."

"I mean it. Hurry up."

"Yes, Mom." Felicia set the sweater aside and held up a black T-shirt, a long-sleeved shirt, a fleecy vest, and a patterned scarf, one at a time. Nothing looked right. Her wardrobe was hopeless. Felicia tossed it all on the floor and flopped down on her bed. In a few minutes she heard her mother's footsteps on the stairs.

"What's going on?"

"I have nothing to wear."

Delia scanned the room. "Why don't you just roll around on the floor and wear whatever you come up with."

"Very funny."

Delia sat down on the bed beside her daughter, stretched and straightened her back. "I know the first day of school is hard, especially when it's a new school."

"If only I had something decent," Felicia said as she sat up.

"Your clothes are fine. We did well shopping with the budget we had." Felicia felt a twinge of guilt. Her single mom worked hard as a secretary—or administrative assistant, as Delia preferred to be called—at a car dealership. "And I know you're not happy that I got transferred here. But it's good for us, easier from a money point of view. It'll work out, you'll see."

Felicia didn't say anything.

"I know Plainsville can't compare with Toronto. Maybe this weekend we can drive over to Collingwood, do some shopping, and go for a swim." Her mother hugged her.

"Perfume." Felicia sniffed.

"Sure. What's wrong with that?"

"It's not the weekend."

"I thought it would be a nice way to start the week."

"Oh."

"Cheerful. Want some?"

"Uh-uh."

They talked in low tones, almost whispering. Felicia's grandmother often slept late. They tried not to disturb her.

"I wish I could be like Nana and sleep in, with nothing to worry about."

"Your Nana has had her share of worries. She's earned her sleep-in time." Delia picked up a sweater from the floor. "Put this on and come down for breakfast. You don't want to be late your first day of school."

Felicia studied the sweater and the T-shirt as her mother left the room. "Maybe the 'layered look' is the best idea." She put on the tee, added the sweater, the vest, and the scarf, and stepped into jeans.

In the kitchen, her mother sipped her coffee from a mug. Felicia stared down at her plate of toast.

"I'm not hungry. I can't eat this."

"Try."

"I can't."

"You're really trying my patience this morning, Lord give me strength."

"My stomach feels funny."

"It's going to feel funnier with nothing in it."

Felicia picked up a piece of toast and bit the corner. It felt like sand on her tongue. She twisted her mouth and closed her eyes.

"At least eat one piece. I'll give you money to buy some lunch, just for today. Tomorrow you pack a sandwich."

After breakfast, Felicia brushed her teeth and studied her face in the bathroom mirror: dark brown eyes, biscuit-brown skin, seeming paler this morning. Her grandmother had fashioned tiny braids in her hair the night before. Felicia wondered what the kids at her new school would think of them, contemplated undoing them, but decided there was not enough time. Besides, she loved the gentle click the beads made when she moved her head. She applied tinted cream to her lips and joined her mother at the front door.

CHAPTER 3
Flower

THE FAMILY sat in a tight circle and shared bread and fruit. Flower liked the cozy safety of the cave. "Pa, can't we stay here?"

"Don't be foolish! How could we live here?" His voice softened as he explained, "Master Chesley is away for business. He won't realize we're gone till he gets back. We have three days. Mustn't waste them." Eldon stood, brushed dirt from his pants. "Finish your meal. I'll scout outside." He parted the branches and disappeared.

Flower ate her apple down to the core. Her mother dug a hole, carefully placed the remains of the fruit in it. "We mustn't leave a trace," she said. Baby brother sat with fat little legs splayed out, supporting him on the dirt floor. Flower rolled a stone toward him, but took it away when he lifted it toward his mouth.

"No, no, Gabriel, that's dirty."

Her father returned and said, "Time to leave. Sun's heading down." They crept from their hiding place and continued the journey. Eldon had memorized the location of the North Star and followed it throughout the night. A sliver of moon provided some light, kept them from walking into trees.

"Why do you keep looking up at the sky?" Flower asked her father.

"Look up yourself." They stopped walking, and Eldon put his hand on her shoulder and tilted her chin. "Over there," he said, pointing. "That group of stars shaped like the long-handled cup that hangs by the barrel—the one we drink out of when we're thirsty."

At first Flower just saw a mass of sparkling light in the dark velvet sky, but as she followed her father's finger, she recognized the shape he was talking about.

"If we keep that ahead of us," he continued, "we'll be heading north. That's the way we want to go—to Canada."

"What's Canada?" asked Flower.

"It's a different country, with different laws. We will be free there."

Flower tried to imagine being free. "What will it be like to be free?"

"Lord, don't you ask a lot of questions. I'm hoping it means I'll get some work and you and Gabriel will get some schooling. We'll manage our own home and our own lives."

They started walking again. Flower's curiosity took another track. "Are there wild beasts here, Papa?"

"It's not the four-legged creatures we need to fear."

"But what if I step on a snake?"

"The snake will be sorry."

"I'm so hungry."

"Just a bit, then." Cleo reached into the sack. They shared bread and water and then resumed their march. The forest thinned, but the terrain remained stony and steep. As the darkness became light, Eldon pointed with satisfaction to the wide ribbon of water far below.

"The Ohio River. We'll cross it tonight."

They searched for cover, settled on a thicket of bushes. Flower continued her mother's bedtime prayers silently in her head as she settled for the day's sleep. They lay beneath a canopy of shrubs, she and her brother nestled between their parents. The branches were thorny, the ground buggy. Flower started to scratch at her bites, but her father slapped her hand. "Keep still!" Flower took in a deep breath and then let it out slowly, trying to ignore the itching. She remembered the icy water of the brook and pictured it flowing over her limbs.

Sunlight filtered through the foliage and, with the breeze, created moving patterns against their faces. It had been easier to sleep in the darkness of the cave.

By early evening, they had left their hiding place, and with relief, stood and stretched their cramped limbs. They ate a few berries and almost finished what remained of the drinking water.

"We'll get more when we reach the river."

"We should be picking fruit. Our food supply is getting smaller."

"Be quick then."

Berries were plucked from the bushes, wrapped in a cloth, and stored in the sack Flower carried. Then they resumed their trek. Eldon continued walking in a northerly direction, the guiding star still visible. Their route, steep in places, took them downhill. Flower started to slide; her father gripped her arm, providing support. When they found themselves on a cleared road, Eldon hurried ahead, stopping where the road split in two directions. A large tree stood in the center of the divided road. Eldon walked up to the tree and embraced it, felt a nail embedded on the right side. "This way."

"How...?"

"Shhh!"

Eldon walked quickly. Cleo and Flower rushed to keep up. They felt uncomfortable on the road, exposed. A fence became visible and then a farmhouse in the distance. The sudden sound of a dog barking caused them to freeze. They drew closer together. Both parents flanked Flower in a protective embrace as they quickly turned and slipped back into the bush alongside the road. They felt safer there, but bumpy ground and tangled brambles slowed their travel.

As the sky lightened, they found another grove of trees and masses of bushes. Together, they added branches, creating shelter to hide them for another day.

CHAPTER 4
Felicia

DELIA DROVE her daughter to school, stopped in front of the low rectangular building. They looked at the entrance and noted three yellow buses parked in the driveway.

"Find out about the bus system."

"Okay."

"I can't be driving you every day."

"I know."

"Especially when you're so tardy."

"I know."

Delia's tone brightened. "You'll meet all the kids, make new friends."

"I know, I know, *I know*."

"Give me a kiss, then, darlin'. Off you go."

Felicia planted a kiss on her mother's cheek and stepped out of the car. At the school door, she turned back to wave good-bye, only to see the back of the car already half a block down the street. Felicia steeled herself and walked with an air of pretend calm through streams of laughing, jostling students to the office.

Inside, a gray-haired woman looked up from her computer screen and smiled over her half glasses at Felicia. "Good morning. How may I help you?"

Felicia reached into her knapsack and presented a piece of paper to the woman, who thanked her and asked her to sit and wait. Felicia sank onto a bench. The breakfast toast squirmed in her stomach. To distract her rebellious digestive system, she stared at everything in this school office: the colorful posters, a wall calendar with puppy-dog illustrations, a vase of yellow flowers.

A woman in a red suit jacket and clicking high heels entered from a rear door and picked up a microphone. Her voice echoed throughout the school, welcoming the students, listing coming tryouts for school teams, choirs, and clubs. The national anthem followed her greetings. Those in the office stood at attention, so Felicia did too.

After that, the woman in the red jacket came over and introduced herself. Her handshake was warm, her smile welcoming.

"I'm Mrs. Mackie, the school principal. You're in Grade Eight, right?" She turned to introduce another girl who had entered the office. "Dorothy will take you to your class." Dorothy looked with interest at Felicia. The two girls left the office and started down the corridor together.

"What did you say your name was?"

"Felicia."

"Wow, that's so pretty."

"Dorothy's nice."

"For an old lady! I don't know what my parents were thinking when they came up with my name. You can call me Dodie. Everybody does."

Felicia glanced at Dorothy as they walked along, noticed her rosy cheeks, her glossy brown braids held in place with butterfly clips.

"I like the way your hair looks."

Dorothy turned to examine Felicia's beaded braids. "I've never seen any like yours up close. How do you make them like that, so tiny?"

"My grandmother did it for me."

They arrived at the classroom door. Dorothy breezed through and Felicia followed, her heart in her throat. She hoped the teacher was nice and wouldn't ask the class to greet her. There was a hum of voices, and nobody stared at her. The teacher put her hand on Felicia's shoulder.

"Attention, everyone! I want you to say hello to your new classmate."

The room became quiet. A few heads swiveled in Felicia's direction. Someone said "Hi."

Felicia tried to keep smiling, ignored her churning stomach. She noticed two girls at the back of the room putting their heads together, one with her hand covering her mouth, whispering.

The teacher's hand squeezed her shoulder. "What's your name, dear?"

"Felicia."

"Lovely. I'm Miss Peabody." Felicia felt herself propelled toward a desk. "Here's your spot. Have a seat."

Felicia sat down with relief. Lined notebooks were distributed. Miss Peabody talked and wrote on the board at the same time. When she underlined a word, the chalk broke in the middle of her sentence. She picked up another piece and continued. Felicia tried to pay attention, but her mind was buzzing. She stared straight ahead at the board, but the words meant nothing to her.

Relax. Stay calm.

Felicia's grandmother had advised her to take deep breaths and count to ten when she was upset, so she inhaled deeply. The room was hot and stuffy. Perspiration began to trickle down her side.

I should have just worn the T-shirt instead of all this other stuff.

But it was too late to change her wardrobe, and since she didn't have a locker yet, she had nowhere to put the extra clothes. Felicia pushed the sleeves of her sweater up to her elbows and felt some relief. The words on the blackboard began to clear. She started to write them down in her notebook, trying not to pay attention to the whispering behind her, but her hand clenched as she heard the distinct words.

"What is it with the teeny weenie braids?"

"Her hair is so fuzzy."

"Kind of weird."

"Totally."

CHAPTER 5
Flower

THE RIVER was not as close as Eldon had thought. They scrambled and scraped their way toward it, but it remained elusive in the distance. Flower's father urged them forward, his breathing labored. "Hurry! Hurry!"

"I'm trying to, Pa."

"Try harder!"

"I'm hurrying as fast as I can."

"Don't talk back to me, child! We need to move!" He grabbed Flower by the arm. Her feet stumbled over one another, and the skin on her arm burned under his grip.

"She's trying. Why are you being so harsh?" asked Cleo.

"The two of you should be listening to me…I'm doing my best to lead you…and getting nothing but sass."

"We're doing our best to follow. We're tired. Let's rest for a bit."

"There's no time, I tell you!" Eldon gave his wife a tug. Startled, she fell in a heap, and the baby began to cry.

"We're your kin, not your slaves. Remember that!" Cleo's eyes blazed up at her husband, then she turned to shush and comfort Gabriel.

Eldon knelt beside his wife. He tried to take her in his arms, but she pushed him away and turned her face to the whimpering baby.

"I'm sorry," he said. "But time is running out…we have to meet a man—I'm not sure where—to take us across the river."

"Will he wait for us?"

"I don't know."

Flower's parents looked steadily at each other, then Eldon helped his wife to her feet. The family started to walk again. Flower had never seen her father act like that. It frightened her to see him frightened. She knew what fear looked like. She had seen and heard things, back where they'd come from. Sometimes there were cries in the night in the shared bunkhouse. She remembered her mother bathing the bleeding backs of two men who had been beaten after they tried to run away. She knew if the family got caught they could face the same punishment. She wondered if there might be a way for them to slip back to the plantation before their absence had been noticed, and before the master knew what they had done. But her father continued to lead them in another direction.

As the sun came up, she heard the swish of moving

water, smelled the dampness of approaching wetland. The ground became muddy, the gumbo sucking at her shoes. Flower unknowingly approached a nest and jumped with alarm as the startled bird shot up into the sky.

"Time for us to make our own nest." Eldon led them to a tangled grove on higher ground, wearily arranged extra branches for cover. The family settled in.

It was late afternoon when Flower awoke. Without disturbing her parents, she slipped out of their hiding place. Within a few minutes she spotted a felled tree, mossy with age. Flower lifted her skirt and perched on it. A small squirrel scurried through the fallen leaves and sat for a moment with his paws up against his face, filling his cheeks with food. Flower held her hand out to him, but he disappeared under a bush.

She wondered how close they were to the river. Perhaps the man was there. It would be wonderful if Flower saw him—she could return to her father and tell him that help was waiting. How relieved he would be! She stood and rearranged her clothing and began to walk.

Her feet were noiseless on the carpeted ground. The forest floor was soft and pliable, the trees far apart, beams of light angling between them. She promised herself she wouldn't go far. Her parents might reach for her in their sleep. They would come awake fearful of where she was.

The sound of the rushing river increased. Suddenly,

just ahead, she saw a man. He was hunched over the water, bringing his cupped hands up to his mouth, drinking from the river as it flowed by. Flower stood motionless. He turned and looked at her.

She had never seen such a monstrous face: charred dark as if from a fire, lumpy and misshapen. Only one eye was open, and it glared at her. She gasped and spun around, tried to run, but wasn't fast enough. Terror made her clumsy. Within a breath, he was upon her, and a cold, wet hand was clamped against her mouth, stifling her desperate cry for her father.

CHAPTER 6
Felicia

FELICIA FOLLOWED the other students down the hallway, hoped they were heading for a cafeteria. Her upset stomach was gone, and now she was hungry. They formed groups and headed in different directions, most of them outdoors. Felicia tried to walk as if she had a destination. The gym and the library were easily found, but where was the cafeteria? If she were back in Toronto, in that comfortable stew of colors and accents, she would be having lunch with Lenore and Rosalee, surrounded by kids she knew, some of them with "fuzzy" hair like hers. Here she felt like a visiting stranger. The whisperers at the back of the classroom had demolished the little confidence she had with their nasty comments about her hair. She overheard someone in the hallway talking about a lunch pit and followed him outside.

She stepped through the doors, and the early September heat hit her like a blast from a furnace. The boy walked toward a central area where many students were congregating—that must be the lunch pit. Felicia swept by that group as if she had someone to meet, someone waiting for her. She considered leaving for home but wasn't sure of the way. There was a white truck with an ice-cream-cone logo on its side parked on the street. Food! Felicia checked her wallet. She had just enough for a hot dog and an ice cream bar.

Felicia purchased her lunch, found leafy shelter beneath a large maple tree, and sank to the grass. She bolted the wiener and bun, then savored the blend of chocolate and ice cream as it melted on her tongue.

The schoolyard was alive with play. There were at least three pickup basketball games, the balls lazily looping through the air, and voices laughing, shouting, calling to each other. Felicia felt alone again, longed to join in, but felt stiff with shyness and encumbered by her mountain of clothing. She wiped the perspiration from her forehead with her sleeve and stayed on the sidelines. It was terrible to sit alone. If only they had stayed in the city, where she had friends. *Now we have to live in geeky old Plainsville.* There had been no discussion about moving. Felicia had not been asked what she would like.

"Hey, Felicity!"

She turned and saw Dodie. "It's Felicia."

"Sorry. Aren't you boiling?"

"Uh, yeah."

Dodie dropped to her knees on the ground, followed by two other girls. "At least you're in the shade."

Dodie introduced Felicia to Renate, who had curly hair and dancing dark eyes, and Sophie, who was red-haired and freckled. "We started to play tetherball, but it was too hot."

"I guess," said Felicia.

"And we have gym after lunch."

"You're kidding!" Felicia wondered how she would manage with her winter wardrobe in the gym. "Outside?"

"Could be. Or, we could complain about the heat, and Miss Peabody might let us play volleyball inside."

"I like volleyball," said Felicia.

"Are you good at sports?" asked Sophie.

"Some. It depends."

"Sophie is an excellent tennis player," said Dodie. "And we all like to ride."

"Bikes?" asked Felicia.

"No, horses!"

She tried to imagine Dodie, Renate, and Sophie riding.

The buzzer rang. The girls stood and brushed grass from their clothing.

"Three more hours!"

"Sophie, please," said Renate, "It's only our first day."

"Sometimes the first time is the worst time. I wish I was at the stable."

"At least we have gym!"

The girls entered the school. The air conditioning provided some relief, but not enough for Felicia, who imagined steam rising from her body.

"Felicia, you're so hot!" said Dodie. "Take some of your stuff off."

"What will I do with it? I don't have a locker yet."

"Take off what's extra," said Renate, "and we'll each wear something." She reached for Felicia's sweater and slid her arm into a sleeve. "This is cool. Where did you get it?"

"In Toronto." Felicia handed her vest to Dodie and the scarf to Sophie. She was left with her T-shirt. "Thanks!"

"No problemo!"

"It's like we're in a fashion show." Renate led the way as they marched together back into the classroom.

CHAPTER 7
Flower

FLOWER BIT down hard on a wet finger.

"Ow! That hurt! Why'd you have to go and do that?"

"You put your hand...over my face!"

"Quiet! To keep you quiet, that's all." He shook his hand in the air and gave it a pained look. "Teeth marks!" Flower started to edge away. He pushed her to the ground. "Where do you think you're going?" She scrambled to her knees and tried to get up. "Stay there." She sank back down to the earth and buried her face in her hands. "What's your name? Where you from? Answer me!"

Flower raised her head and then lowered it. His face was too horrid to look at. "I don't know."

"What do you mean, you don't know? Everybody knows their name."

"My Pa is going to whup you." Flower hoped her father would hear them and rescue her.

"Where's your Pa, then?"

Flower looked up and beyond the man. "Here he

comes." She could see her father striding toward them through the trees, a large stick in his raised hand. She ran and clung to him.

"Don't go pushing my child about!"

"I didn't mean any harm."

"It surely looked like you did."

"I wasn't going to hurt her. Please, I'm a slave on the run. I'm waiting for someone to help me cross the river."

"Waiting? How long?"

"Today is four."

Flower's father dropped the stick and looked toward the river. "We must talk."

Cleo, with Gabriel bouncing in her arms, rushed to embrace Flower when they returned. The hug was paired with a scolding. "Where have you been? You must stay close." She noticed the stranger following behind. "Is this the man who is going to help us?"

"No. He's waiting too," Eldon said.

"Oh no." Cleo's voice was soft with disappointment as she turned to greet the newcomer. Flower turned her face away, heard her mother gasp. "You're hurt!" Cleo stepped closer and studied the side of his head. "Let me see to it." She handed the baby to her daughter.

"There's a safer place down by the river," said the stranger.

The family gathered their few belongings and

followed him to the sheltered spot. There, Cleo tore a rag in two. She dipped one section in the river and gently washed the man's wound, removing the crusted blood from his face, then covered his lesion with the other. His swollen eye slowly opened, and he looked at his nurse with gratitude. Flower carried her brother, sang quietly to him, and wondered how her mother could stand to touch such ugliness.

After, they sat together and shared their food. Eldon said, "Tell us your story."

The man sat quietly as if to collect his thoughts, then began. "My name is Samuel. I come from a plantation in Georgia. The master was cruel. He treated us so bad."

"His name?"

"Logan."

Eldon nodded and Samuel continued. "He sold my sister. She cried and cried, and tried to hold on to me, but she was pulled away. We'd been together forever; she was the only family I had. It was too much for me. I couldn't stand being there any longer. I decided to run away. I didn't succeed, as you can see." Samuel swallowed and looked at the ground. "After I was caught and returned to him, he called everyone together to watch. Then he nailed my ear to a post, drew a knife, and sliced it off."

Poor Samuel! Flower's fingers touched her right ear—grateful it was still there—then her mouth, as she felt a rising nausea. She closed her eyes and tried to close her mind against the dreadful images there.

"I stayed for one day, then ran again," continued Samuel.

"Terrible, terrible," said Cleo.

Eldon brooded. "We need to leave this place. I have to wonder if the man who is supposed to help us is going to come, or whether we should try to find our own way to cross the river."

"The river is deep and fast," said Samuel. "We should look for a place that's easier to cross."

"Perhaps tonight the man will come," said Cleo, but her voice was wistful.

CHAPTER 8
Felicia

FELICIA STEPPED down from the school bus and walked up the driveway, carrying her extra clothing. Her grandmother sat on the porch.

"What's that you're carrying? Have you been to a rummage sale? Or shopping?"

"I wish." Felicia flopped down on the steps and dropped her bundle. "I'm so hot!"

"The world is heating up, there's no doubt. We're paying for our sins: avarice and greed."

"Don't those two words mean the same thing?"

"What of it?"

"You're repeating yourself."

"Of course. I meant to…for emphasis." Florence changed the subject. "You managed to organize a seat on the bus."

"Yup. No problem."

"Good. How about the school? Were the kids friendly?"

Felicia didn't want to repeat the words whispered behind her back in the classroom. "I met three girls. They helped me out with all this stuff." She described the sharing and the way they had all sashayed into the classroom wearing her clothes.

Florence laughed. "They sound like good kids. Now, if Delia's job works out as well as your school, we'll be just fine."

"I have homework, too, you'll be glad to know."

"What kind of homework are you getting on the first day of school? Weren't you able to keep up?"

"Don't worry, Nana, I can keep up. We're supposed to write about what we did this summer."

"'How I spent my summer vacation.' Your teacher doesn't sound very imaginative. So what are you going to write about? Our trip to Niagara Falls?"

"No, not that. I'll think of something." Felicia gathered her discarded clothing. "I'm going to change into some shorts."

"Wait up. Give me a hand. That's a good girl." Florence pushed herself from the chair and stood stiffly. "This blasted knee." She placed a hand on her granddaughter's shoulder, and together they walked into the house. Florence settled in a large lounge chair, moved a lever on its side, and a part of the chair flipped up to support her feet. As her head tilted back, she pointed the remote control at the television set in the corner. The screen expanded and noise filled the room.

Her granddaughter was not an admirer of the game show that filled the screen. "How can that woman be so excited about a refrigerator? Why doesn't she save her pride and just go out and buy one?"

"Maybe she can't afford to."

Felicia considered her grandmother's answer, and her intense focus on the program. "Nana, do you want a new refrigerator?"

"No, dear."

"But if you needed one, could you afford to buy it, or would you have to make a fool of yourself on some stupid TV show like this poor loser woman is doing?"

"I could buy one. I'd have to make payments, I guess. But I wouldn't mind being on this program either. It's fun trying to answer the questions. I'm pretty good at it."

"I still think it's not dignified." But Florence's attention had shifted back to the set, so Felicia retreated to her bedroom. It was a small space with shelves on one wall from floor to ceiling. The opposite wall had a window. Felicia perched on her narrow bed and gazed out.

The garden was large and unruly—flowers and vegetables grew beside each other. There was no apparent effort at design, but the space was radiant with color. Beyond the garden, she could see the neighbor's orchard, and in the distance, broad fields, flat, then undulating to the base of large blue-green hills. Felicia recognized the beauty, yet she missed the brick buildings and busy streets of the city. She wondered what her friends were doing.

The telephone was located on a wall in the kitchen. Felicia started down the stairs. "Nana, can I use the phone?"

"Is that for long distance?"

"Yes."

"Normally, I'd say no, 'cause it's expensive this time of day. But I know you're missing your friends, so just fifteen minutes."

Felicia settled at the kitchen table and called her friend Lenore.

"Felish! What's happening?"

"Not much. What's happening with you?"

"Rosalee's here. We're beading bracelets and watching Y and R."

"I wish I was there with you. I haven't seen it in so long, I can't remember the story."

"It's so good. Lance is falling in love with Marie, but Marie has this past secret, and she knows if he finds out, he'll hate her."

"What's the terrible secret?"

"We're not sure, but we think it's because her parents aren't her real parents. She was a stray left at somebody's front door. Her real dad's a killer, and he's just escaped from prison."

"I can relate. Today I feel like a stray left at somebody's front door."

"Felish! Can you come back here? Come and live with us."

"I have a mom and grandma, remember? But I miss you guys."

"We miss you too. Come down and see us. You can stay at my place."

"Really?"

"Duh! Of course."

"Felicia, time's up!" Her grandmother called out. "Did you hear me?"

"Yes."

"Turn the oven on for me, that's a good girl. When it gets to be 350, put the meatloaf in. It's sitting on the counter. And pare the carrots."

Felicia turned and looked at the preparations for dinner—the meat in a loaf pan, a pile of orange vegetables. "Okay."

"Then come and join me, sweetie, when you're finished. This program is fun."

CHAPTER 9
Flower

THE FAMILY searched for food as they prepared to cross the river. Berried bushes provided most of their meals, the bread now long gone. Samuel caught two squirrels. He roasted them in a pit at night so that the smoke would not be visible. Flower ate her share but felt a pang of remorse, remembering the charm of the busy little animal she had admired just three days before.

As they sat with their shared meal, Flower tried not to look in Samuel's direction. If his bandage rag slipped away, she would catch a glimpse of his grisly wound.

"Not much meat on a squirrel," Samuel said.

"Yes, next time catch us a bear." Sometimes Flower's father joked to make people feel better. He was rewarded with a rare smile from Samuel.

After their meager dinner, they walked to the water to wash the food from their hands. Cleo looked with foreboding at the dark water flowing by. "Not one of us is able to swim."

"The raft is coming along."

"It's taking a long time."

"No. It's going well. Stop fussing, woman!"

"I'm not fussing. I'm just worried."

"Worry is a waste of time." Eldon embraced his wife and patted her back affectionately. "Find us some more vines, and we'll get back to work."

Flower watched her parents and wanted to be included in their hug, wanted to run over and place herself between them, as she used to do when she was little. Instead, she squeezed her brother, who rewarded her with a wet kiss on her cheek.

Samuel dragged another log as they walked to the sheltered cove. He was not as strong as her father, who pulled the logs along with ease. Eldon helped him place it alongside the others.

"We have six of almost equal length."

"Six more would make it right."

"If only we had an axe."

"There would be noise then, and someone would hear us."

They all turned briefly to look over their shoulders, a nervous reflex. Eldon regarded the small craft. "It's starting to look seaworthy."

"As if we knew what we were doing," added Samuel.

"You should be proud," Cleo said. "You've never made anything like this before."

Flower looked down at the rectangle of logs with less respectful eyes. To her, it just looked like a jumble of mismatched trees, barely held together with vines, not capable of carrying them anywhere, especially across the river. "I'm not going to get on that."

Her father gave her a stern look. "You'll do what you're told when the time comes."

At the plantation they'd escaped from, they had spent their lives doing what they were told. Flower recognized that at least her father was giving orders for her own safety, not to work her to exhaustion. Her thoughts returned to Aunty. Flower hoped she wasn't being given extra chores now that they were gone and not able to share the daily labor.

Gabriel began to whimper and held out his arms to his mother, who lifted him into hers. "I'll feed him, and then we should be bedding down. The sun will soon make things bright."

"I'm hungry too," said Flower.

"Have some more berries and a sip of water, then settle in."

"I want bread."

"You know there isn't any. Hush now, child." Cleo took her daughter's hand, and together they started for their shelter. Eldon and Samuel began to lay leafy branches over the raft to hide it.

Suddenly, they heard a dog barking. Even the baby lifted his head. Another bark, then two dogs together, perhaps more. They sounded far away, but they were moving. Samuel began to moan.

Eldon looked at the water. "It's time."

"How can we? It's not finished." Samuel hung his head. "It's too late."

"Hurry now! It's our only chance!"

Samuel started to moan again. "Oh, Lord…"

Eldon grabbed the other man by the shoulders and said, "The Lord helps those who help themselves. Remember?"

"I'm so afraid."

"Come on. Let's get going."

They uncovered the raft and returned to the task of lashing the remaining logs together. The vines were in a heap. Flower reached into the tangle, handed the shoots to her father and Samuel as fast as she could. The men tugged and twisted, weaving the lumber together, making the joins as tight as possible. Cleo sat and nursed Gabriel, murmuring to him to try to block out the yowling of the approaching animals.

Soon they could hear men's voices, as well as the pack of dogs. Eldon and Samuel eased the raft into the river and helped the others huddle in the center of it. Both men stepped aboard, each with a long pole. Together they planted them against the ground and pushed off into the current.

CHAPTER 10
Felicia

AT THE END of the first week of school, the three girls talked Felicia into coming with them to the stable.

"You can watch us ride."

"Or, you can ride yourself."

"No. She can't without taking a lesson."

"Do you want to have a lesson?" asked Dodie.

"Um…I don't know. I have to talk to my mom."

"Let Felicia see what it's like. Maybe she'll hate the place."

Dodie laughed. "Are you kidding? She'll love it."

Felicia wasn't so sure. Horses were big animals. What if she got in the way and one accidentally stepped on her foot? And couldn't horses sense when you were nervous? What if she got on one and it didn't behave and decided all on its own to gallop into town with her still in the saddle? She didn't want to be seen as the clumsy "city slicker" who didn't know her way around a barn.

"We all love it," enthused Sophie.

"It's so much fun," added Renate.

"Okay," said Felicia. "I'll come."

The barn was located on the edge of town, a thirty-minute walk from the school. Felicia followed the girls inside to a large tack room. She looked around at saddles on brackets and reins neatly strapped together hanging from hooks while the other girls changed into riding clothes. They zippered chaps over their pants, then lugged the gear out into the corridor between the stalls.

"So far, you all look like Wonder Woman."

"The saddles aren't that heavy. Here, try one."

Felicia picked up a saddle and sank almost to her knees, pretending to collapse with the weight. She replaced it on a post as the girls laughed at her theatrics.

"Now for the best part," said Renate.

"What?"

"We go and get our horses."

"From where?"

"The field. Come with us." She picked up a halter and lead rope.

Felicia trailed behind the girls and watched as they persuaded their horses to accept the halter. Dodie's horse was the only one to resist. Every time she approached him, he wandered away.

"This calls for severe measures," said Dodie.

"What are you going to do?" asked Felicia.

43

"Bribe him." Dodie lifted a peppermint from her pocket. "Look what I have, Cecil." The horse ambled over, lowered his head for the treat, and Dodie slipped on the halter.

Back in the barn, Felicia watched the girls prepare their mounts for the lesson. As they strapped on their helmets, their teacher arrived.

"What's keeping you all? We could have started five minutes ago."

"Cecil took forever."

"Too much visiting, I think."

"Francine, this is Felicia. She's come to watch us today." Renate made the introduction.

"Hello, Felicia, and welcome. You want to watch the lesson? The best place to do that is over there."

Felicia sat on an old kitchen chair at one end of the arena and watched the action from behind a barrier. By the middle of the lesson, she stood and leaned against the top board as her new friends trotted along the sides of the enclosure. Felicia enjoyed the sound of hooves thumping and leather saddles creaking.

"Aren't they finished yet?"

Felicia recognized the voices behind her. These were the whisperers from the back of the class. "Hi."

They were slender and attractive. Felicia knew the taller, prettier one was called Ashley. She couldn't remember the name of the other one. Their riding attire looked expensive.

Ashley wore cream-colored jodhpurs that tapered into long, glossy boots. Neither girl said hello.

Felicia turned back to the lesson, still listening to their conversation as she watched the activity in the arena.

"Do you think Renate will ever figure out where her heels are?"

"She has all those stupid curls sticking out under her helmet."

"Look at Dodo's braids flapping all over the place."

"Then there's poor Sophie's complexion. She must have a million freckles."

"That's what happens when you stay out in the sun too long, *and* you have carrot-red hair and pasty skin."

"Yeah. Or else you get a *really* dark tan."

Their remarks degenerated into giggles. Felicia stood like a soldier, her back rigid with contempt. If only she could think of some witty, scathing remark, put them in their place, let them feel what it's like to be hurt. But she remained silent.

The lesson ended, and the riders led their horses back into the barn.

Ashley said to Felicia, "Are you helping out today?"

"No, just watching."

"You should stick around, see some real riding."

This girl was too much. "But that would be *really* boring."

Ashley glared at Felicia, "You don't know…"

Francine interrupted. "Ashley! Cynthia! What are you doing just standing around? Why aren't your horses tacked up? I've got things to do if you don't."

Felicia was glad to see the two girls herded back into the barn by their instructor, who continued to chastise them the whole way.

CHAPTER 11
Flower

THE LITTLE RAFT scraped the bottom of the river when the men stepped aboard. Eldon hopped off, pushed the craft into deeper water, and climbed back on. It briefly sank sideways with the additional weight but stayed afloat. Water swirled across the surface. Cleo and Flower knelt in the middle, Gabriel shrieking between them. Eldon and Samuel stood at opposite corners, using their long poles to push farther out into the middle of the river.

The two men struggled to maintain their balance as the raft dipped and bobbed and turned in circles. Cleo gripped her infant and held fast to the wood beneath her with her other hand. Flower wanted to cling to her mother, but instead dug her fingers deep between two lengths of log.

Cleo said, "Hold on, daughter, hold on! Don't let go!"

The two men tried to time the plunge of the poles into the water, saying "heave!" with each attempt.

Now they could hear triumphant shouts. Three men

on horseback called out across the water. "Come back in the name of the law!" A pack of hounds bayed and barked, running back and forth along the shore. Some plunged into the water.

"Ha! Will you look at that? A whole bunch of them."

"The more the merrier. More money for us."

"Come back here! Don't make us come and get you. You'll regret it."

Eldon tried to override the threats with his own voice of encouragement. "Keep going! Keep trying—we must keep trying!"

They had almost managed to reach the middle of the river. The water was deeper; their poles no longer touched bottom but moved uselessly, banging against the little craft. Samuel tried to plunge his pole down to the river bottom, lost his balance, and dropped the pole into the river. He watched it float away, then crumpled in a heap of despair.

"We're done for."

Eldon tried to use his pole as a paddle, but it was too thin. He groaned with the effort of directing the raft. They had reached a bend in the river where the current slowed, delaying their progress and sending them back in the wrong direction.

The men on shore yelled, "Try and get away, will you? Think you know how to make a boat? Hah!"

"We can just set ourselves down here real comfortable and wait for them to wash back up on shore."

The dogs barked with increasing hysteria. A few of them started swimming out to the raft. The men laughed harder. "Go get 'em! Bring 'em in for us!"

The dogs were getting close. Flower could see their snarling jaws. She imagined one sinking its teeth into her leg and pulling her into the water, dragging her back to disaster.

Her father shouted to Samuel. "Get in the water. It's our only chance."

"I can't swim!"

"Nor can I. We can hold on and kick our legs."

"But..."

"Now!" Eldon leaped into the water and, after a brief moment, so did Samuel. They clung to one side of the raft and kicked hard with their feet. The raft was lighter without their weight and moved forward.

"Don't go drowning now! We don't want our wages reduced!" The men jeered at first, but as the raft moved slowly away from them toward the opposite shore, their laughter stopped.

"Damn! They're getting away!"

"Get back here if you know what's good for you!"

"You're making things worse for yourself!"

Their voices became fainter. There was silence, then a

blast of firearms. Gunshots danced on the surface, but far behind them.

"Get down!" Eldon's warning was unnecessary. Cleo lay on top of Gabriel.

Flower turned to look at her father and Samuel, but only their fingers were visible, clinging to the edge. She could hear their labored breathing. "Pa," she said. He didn't answer.

The gunfire stopped. The sound of barking dogs grew fainter. Cleo raised her head. "The far shore—we're almost there! Husband, take heart! We're almost there."

Samuel said, "Thank heavens." Water poured into his mouth, and he started to choke and spit.

Eldon tried to touch bottom but it was still too deep. "Keep going," he said.

Cleo and Flower clung to the wet logs, touched their foreheads together with relief.

No one saw the rock. The sudden force of the impact shattered the raft into pieces. Flower didn't have time to cry out. She flew up into the air, then into icy blackness, her mouth and nose filling with water. Her skirt billowed about her, clinging to her legs, weighing her down. Instinctively, she thrashed her arms and legs and tried to bring her face to the surface, but it was too hard. She began to sink.

CHAPTER 12
Felicia

AFTER SUPPER, Felicia sat at the kitchen table with her mother and grandmother, the unwashed dishes still at their elbows. Earlier in the day, Florence had made a batch of chili sauce, and the air was fragrant with the sweet aroma of brown sugar, vinegar, and tomatoes. The filled jars sat glowing on the counter.

"The sauce smells delicious, Mom," said Delia. "Looks good too. Are you worn out now?"

"No. Just my knee is a little stiff from all that standing."

"Felicia, you can do the dishes for your grandmother."

"Don't I always?"

"Excuse me?" Delia raised an eyebrow.

"Yes, you do," said Florence, "and I thank you. Myself, I've spent many a day doing chores, with hardly a 'thank you' that I can remember." She turned to her daughter and asked, "How's the new job going?"

"Pretty good. Mr. Abbot says he appreciates my 'organizational skills.'"

"You've always been a neat and organized person," Florence said.

"Almost anal," said Felicia.

"What! Where does she get these words?"

"Everybody knows what 'anal' means, Mom."

"What does it mean?"

"It means sometimes you can be too neat and organized, maybe a little obsessive."

"I am *not* obsessive."

"Felicia, you should always be polite to your elders. That never goes out of style. Now tell us about your day," said Florence.

"It was okay. I went to the saddle club after school and watched my friends ride." Felicia felt odd using the term "friends." Were they really her friends, or were they just being nice? "They want me to ride, too."

"Did you tell them we are working people, not part of the horsey set?"

"Mom, we didn't discuss family finances."

"Don't be such a sassy little girl."

"I'm not a little girl, and you're the one who asked if I told them about how much money we have."

Florence said, "Maybe there is a good sports program at your school."

The telephone rang, interrupting their discussion. It was Dodie.

"Felicia, what homework do we have? I left my notes at school."

"Math." Felicia reached behind her chair and opened her backpack. "Just a sec…it's chapter three, page twenty-five, exercises one through seven. Have you got your book?"

"Ugh! No!"

"I'll read them to you."

"That would save my life. Peabody will target me tomorrow for sure."

After Felicia had finished dictating the assignment, Dodie asked, "What did you think of the barn?"

"It was okay. Is Francine mean to you?"

"No. She's cool. She just yells so we can hear her. It's noisy in the arena."

"Do the horses bite you sometimes?"

"They can bite each other. Cecil is really gentle. He's my sweetie. I've been riding him for three years."

"Are there any teams at the school?"

"The boy's hockey team, and the girls' volleyball team, and then there's gym. And if you have an outside sport, like swimming or tennis or riding, you get extra credit."

"Oh yeah?"

"Also, with riding, there's a special rider's program, and if you help with that, then it gives you better marks in social studies."

"I don't think I could afford a horse."

"You don't have to buy one. Francine has school horses. That's what we do. There are also secondhand clothes at the tack shop—boots and riding pants. Plus you'll need a helmet, of course."

"I thought you each had your own horse."

"We wish."

Felicia decided to present this proposal to her mother, but Delia listened with barely contained impatience. "I told you before. We're not the type of people to be riding horses."

"What type is that, Mom?"

"You know what I mean!"

"No, I don't."

Delia sighed and looked at her own mother.

Florence said, "Felicia, be courteous to your mother. She just wants what's best for you. Now tell us about these girls. They're your new friends, and they like to ride…"

"Yes."

"And they've asked you to ride with them?"

"Yes."

"Has anyone else invited you to join them in doing something?"

"No." Felicia looked down at her plate.

"Not yet," said Delia.

"Is this riding safe?"

"Yes. The horses are gentle, and we're in an arena with a teacher."

Florence paused to sip her tea. "How much does it cost?"

Felicia responded, and the amount seemed to sit suspended in the air as her mother and grandmother stared into space.

Delia sat with her chin resting on her right hand and said nothing. Florence had another sip of tea. Her swallow was audible in the silence of the kitchen.

"Please, Mom."

Delia folded her hands together. "I guess I'm going to have to come to this place and see it for myself."

At the end of their conversation, Felicia sat trying to imagine riding a horse. She wondered if Dodie might share Cecil with her, since he was so gentle. But then they couldn't ride together. The clatter of dishes intruded on her thoughts.

Delia was standing at the sink. "Hey, Mom, I'll help!" Felicia opened a drawer and lifted out a towel. "Where's Nana?"

"Watching television."

"Her favorite thing to do."

"One of them."

"Do you miss your friends, Mom?"

"Oh sure, but I think our move will work out. We'll

keep our old friends and make some new ones, and it's nice to be able to afford to rent a house rather than an apartment. Don't you think?"

"I guess."

"Your grandmother loves having a garden." As she talked, Delia scrubbed the counter from one end to the other. Then she squeezed water out of the dishrag, folded it into a wet rectangle, and placed it on the edge of the sink. Her daughter watched this activity and said, "You're doing a good job—really neat and well organized."

Delia flicked a bubble of soap at her daughter before drying her hands.

CHAPTER 13
Flower

FLOWER FELT a strong hand grab her hair and yank her to the surface. She gasped for air. Samuel held on to a log and pushed Flower against it. They floated this way briefly, and then Samuel said, "Kick your feet."

Their efforts were feeble; they kicked as silently as they could, without splashing, but with enough strength to move them slowly toward the Ohio shore. When Samuel's feet touched bottom, he tried to wade in and fell twice. Flower stumbled along with him. They crawled the final few yards, then flopped onto dry land. Flower lay face down on the dirt and stones and vomited the river water out of her body, the sour fluid scalding her throat.

Panic overrode her exhaustion. "Pa! Ma!" She pushed herself up on her elbow, wailing their names into the empty air.

"Hush! We don't know who might hear us!"

Flower lay back down on her side and cried like an infant. "I want my Ma and Pa, and my baby brother."

"We'll look for them." Samuel was short of breath. "In a moment we'll search."

When they felt strong enough to stand, Samuel led the way into a grove of trees. He said to Flower, "Stay here and don't move." Then he returned to where they had come ashore and, with a leafy branch, brushed away the evidence of their footprints.

Flower watched from her hiding place in the trees. When he came back, she asked, "Aren't we safe here?"

"Don't know."

There was no sign of her family. The only sounds were the rushing of the water and the cries of birds overhead. Flower began to shiver in her soaking wet clothing, her mind a storm of distress. Was she alone in the world now? There had been children without parents back at the plantation. They were fed and housed, but when they needed comfort or affection, did they get much? Some of the women, especially her mother and Aunty Lizzie, had been kind, but that wasn't nearly enough. Flower remembered the unattended runny noses, coughs, and cries in the night. Her shivers became spasms of fear.

Samuel looked down at his young charge and rubbed her back. "We must keep moving." He looked in both directions. "But which way?"

"You don't know what you're doing."

"I'm doing the best I can. What do you know?"

"My Pa would know." Flower didn't want to be with Samuel but stumbled after him. Though he had saved her life, the memory of their first meeting remained vivid—how he had grabbed her, thrown her to the ground, shouted at her. If she displeased him, would he behave like that again?

Samuel stopped and looked about. "We're walking in the wrong direction, heading back against the river flow. We should be going with it. Turn around. The others should be here somewhere."

Flower couldn't stop her dark thoughts. *Unless they're still in the water…*

"Papa," she called out softly.

"Hush, I tell you!"

Flower began to cry. "Papa…I want my Papa!"

Samuel wheeled around, grabbed her by the shoulders, and began to shake her.

"Stay quiet when I tell you to!"

Flower wept through chattering teeth. "Papa!"

"Flower?"

They stood quiet for a brief moment. Flower answered, "Pa?"

"Flower! Stay where you are, daughter! I'll find you!"

They could hear movement through the trees. Ignoring Eldon's command, they moved forward to meet him. Flower threw herself against her father, and he held her gratefully.

Flower was afraid to ask. "Ma?"

"She's safely hidden, with the babe. Come, follow me."

Eldon led them to a sheltered spot, deep within a thicket of bushes and evergreens. Cleo sat with her back against a tree. She jumped up and rocked her daughter in her arms. "I thought I'd never see you again."

"We're all together now. I think we should go further inland," said Eldon, "away from the river."

"We're so tired," protested Cleo. "We've had no sleep."

"Safe. We must be safe," said Eldon. "We'll find a safe spot and build a fire to warm us. Then sleep will be sweet."

They walked for hours, stopping only once when Flower dropped to the ground with exhaustion. She fell asleep instantly, came awake when she felt her father lift her close to the warmth of a small fire. They huddled around it and tried to ignore their hunger.

CHAPTER 14
Felicia

AS THE GIRLS walked together to the barn, Renate asked, "What do you all think of joining the drama club?"

"What for?" asked Dodie.

"For fun, that's what for!"

"Fun for you," said Sophie. "I'm too shy to be in a play, with everyone looking at me."

"But being in a play might be good for your shyness," suggested Felicia. "You'd get to be more confident."

"Maybe there'll be a musical like *Grease* or something and we could get singing parts." Renate remained enthused. "Besides, Josh and Matt want us to join. Josh is writing a play. He told me he wants us to be in it."

"Oh yeah?"

"And Matthew is so funny."

"He is?" asked Felicia, who had never talked to him.

"Hilarious."

"Anyway, there's a drama club meeting tomorrow. I think we should go."

"Let's put on a show…" Dodie started to sing. The others joined in as they made a melodic entrance to the barn.

Delia had left work early as planned so that she could join Felicia at the saddle club. When she arrived, she stood with Felicia at the end of the arena and watched the riding class. Felicia looked over her shoulder twice, willing Ashley and Cynthia not to appear. More mean comments from them would surely ruin any plans for riding. Delia would be confirmed in her notion that she and her daughter didn't belong to the "horsey set."

At the end of the lesson, Francine came directly over to the two of them and shook Delia's hand. "Welcome to Green Hills." Francine led Delia on a tour, showing with pride the tack room, feed room, and her small office at one end of the building. They returned to the students who were brushing their horses. Dodie's mount raised his tail and deposited a steaming mound on the concrete floor.

"We keep a clean barn. That's meant for the manure pile." Francine lifted a bedding fork off a hook and transferred the future fertilizer to a wheelbarrow. Dodie swept the floor clean. "I hope Felicia can join the group," said Francine. "I have the perfect horse for her."

"Which one?" asked Dodie.

"Give me a minute. I'll show you." Francine slid open a stall door at the far end of the barn and led a horse toward them. "Isn't she precious? I've been working with her for a few weeks."

"Can I ride her?" asked Renate.

"You have Calvin to ride." Francine turned to Felicia and Delia. "Come and say hello."

Delia raised her hands and shook her head, but Felicia stepped forward and gently touched the horse's face.

"Where did she come from?" asked Renate.

"How old is she?"

Francine clipped cross ties to the halter, removed the lead rope, and said, "Hold on, I'll be right back." She returned with a photo showing a sorry looking, emaciated horse, its head hanging, every rib and both hipbones painfully evident.

Even Delia was amazed. "This can't be the same animal!"

"Yes, it is. I found her at a sale, rescued her from a farm that had been impounded by the courts. A number of horses were there in terrible condition, so neglected. Some were immediately put down."

"How could anyone be so mean?" asked Sophie.

"It's hard to imagine, isn't it? But she's come along nicely. I've been training her, and she's wonderful, a real treasure."

Felicia looked into soft, brown eyes, and it seemed the horse returned her gaze. "What's her name?"

"I'm calling her Morning Star because of the star shape on her forehead. And when I went to bring her home—it was early in the morning—I could still see the moon, very faintly, and a large, bright star in the sky beside it."

CHAPTER 15
Flower

THERE WAS no sound to warn them, only the sense that they were no longer alone. Flower heard her mother's soft moan of fear, opened her eyes, and saw a tall man looking down at them. He was dressed entirely in black, with a black hat on his head. Beneath the brim, his pale face was lean and craggy, the light from the fire deepening the shadows beneath his eyes.

Her father managed only one word—"Mercy."

The stranger stepped forward, moving into the firelight. "Yes, 'tis God's mercy—he has delivered you safely to me." He noted the condition of the group assembled at his feet, their sodden clothes and shivering bodies. "Did Jonah's craft sink, take on water?"

"We met no Jonah. We made our own raft. It hit a rock and broke apart."

"Can you walk?"

They struggled to their feet.

The stranger told them he was Noah Pemberton, a

Quaker and a friend. He led them up a stony incline and through a field to a narrow frame house, light spilling out from an open doorway. A woman holding a lamp stood on the threshold. She, too, was dressed in black, with a small cap on her head concealing her hair. Her face had the same sharp angles as the man's, but it was smaller, more birdlike.

"Oh my," she said as she observed the ragtag group assembled before her. "Come in, come in." She held out her hand and motioned for them to come forward.

No one moved. They stood sodden and hesitant, unsure about entering a white person's home.

"Round the back then—men to the stable and mother and children to the kitchen. You can change out of those clothes. Come now, before you expire." She herded them round to the back of the house and introduced herself as Sarah Pemberton. She helped Cleo sink into a chair, cooing over Gabriel as he was released from his sling.

Flower felt nimble fingers remove her wet clothes, a washrag scrub her face and hands. "There. That will do for now. You can bathe properly tomorrow." Sarah lifted a cotton gown over Flower's head and helped her find the sleeves.

When they were dressed, she invited them to sit at the kitchen table. Mrs. Pemberton lifted a loaf of bread from a box and began to slice it. "There's cheese coming. Please help yourself."

Flower tried to copy her mother's delicate nibbling, though she wanted to tear into her share. Her father's first swallow was accompanied by a long sigh.

After their simple meal, the men returned to the stable, and Mrs. Pemberton led Flower, her mother, and baby brother to an attic room at the top of the house. They barely noted the luxury of bed linen and mattress beneath their exhausted bodies as they fell into a deep sleep.

In the morning, Flower was reluctant to wake up. Half asleep, she clung to her mother and begged her to stay in bed, but Cleo refused. "I hear noises below. That kind woman is making us a meal."

Footsteps on the stairs, then Mrs. Pemberton's head appeared through the opening in the floor. She grunted with the effort of carrying a jug and basin. Cleo jumped up to take them from her hands.

"There. You and the children can wash." In a few minutes she was back with an armful of clothing. The dress meant for Flower was too large; the hem dragged along the floor. "We see few children, but this dress can be altered to fit."

Clean and dressed, Cleo, Gabriel, and Flower descended the narrow stairs. Eldon was seated at the long pine table. Noah Pemberton sat at the far end, and his wife brought them bowls of steaming tea. Sarah motioned for the rest of the family to sit down.

"You should be seated, and I will bring food to the table," Cleo said.

"A kind thought, but I know my own kitchen—and I'm amazed you can put one foot in front of the other after such a long trek."

Noah addressed Flower's father. "Tell us of your journey and of yourself."

Eldon set a piece of paper on the table. It was a letter he had been carrying, folded neatly but still wet. Noah opened it carefully, set fine wire glasses on the end of his long nose, and began to read.

CHAPTER 16
Felicia

FELICIA STOOD in front of a mirror, gazed at her image, snapped her helmet firmly into place, and shook her head in wonder. She listened as Francine negotiated the price of everything with the shop owner.

"The boots have been polished, but you can still see the wear," Francine said.

"Those were very expensive boots."

"Not anymore. And these pants have seen better days."

"Originally top of the line."

"There's a thread loose on the side seam."

"Oh, give me a break!"

After the wrangling, Delia presented her credit card, and the transaction was complete. They exited the store, Felicia carrying a large bag. Francine led them to the local bakery where they ordered mugs of tea and muffins, still warm from the oven.

"There. You're all set," said Francine as they settled at a round table.

Felicia smiled at her riding teacher. Her mother spoke for both of them. "Thank you for helping us at the shop. I'm not very good at bargaining. I think I always end up paying more whenever I try."

"No problem. Jane's a friend of mine, and she gets lots of her inventory from my students." She asked Felicia, "Are you all excited now that you have the gear?"

"Yes."

"Nervous?"

"Yes."

"That's okay."

"Felicia is good at sports," said Delia. "But I worry. I think it must be very different to work with an animal. You can't just rely on your own efforts; you have to hope the horse is going to cooperate."

"Absolutely! That's why riding is so special—it's the working relationship that develops between horse and rider."

"Will this horse she's going to be riding behave itself?"

Francine didn't laugh at this question. "We're going to work together, Felicia and I, because I think this horse is worth the effort." She turned to her student. "Are you ready to do that?"

"Sure!"

After their tea, they got in the car and followed Francine's pickup truck back to the stable. Felicia changed into her riding pants and boots while Francine brought Morning Star in from the field. Delia kept a respectful distance as Felicia began the process of learning how to groom and ready the horse for her ride.

"Talk to her while you brush," said Francine. "Let her get to know you. While you're doing that, have a good look at her. See if she has any sores or swelling."

"Where would she have swelling?"

"On her legs."

"There's a mark here on her rump."

Francine took a look. "Someone's nipped her. Nothing serious."

"Oh no! Poor Star!"

"It happens. They push each other around. She has to learn her place as part of the herd."

Francine showed Felicia how to lift Morning Star's hooves, one at a time, and pick them clean. The saddle was next. Felicia hoisted it on top of a quilted pad and fastened the girth strap, which ran from one side of the saddle to the other, under the horse's belly. The bit and bridle presented more of a challenge. Francine instructed Felicia to place the bit in the horse's mouth and the bridle straps across her nose and over her ears. All the while, the horse stood quietly and tossed her head only once.

In the arena, Francine did a final check, tightened the girth strap, then led Star to the mounting block, and Felicia swung on. With a line clipped to the halter, Francine led horse and rider in a large circle.

"How does that feel?"

"High up."

"You'll get used to that. She's actually not a very big horse." Francine's strong hands gripped Felicia's booted feet and realigned them in the stirrups. "Heels down." She pushed her student's lower legs against the horse's sides. "Hug your horse. That's better. Now, pick up the reins."

By the end of the lesson, Felicia had trotted in a circle on the lunge line, then down the long side of the arena on her own. Finally, she walked the perimeter of the arena, waving at her mother. Delia followed them back into the barn and watched as Felicia removed tack and toweled the horse. Star was given a carrot for her efforts, her soft muzzle grazing Felicia's palm as she received the treat.

Dodie, Renate, and Sophie arrived.

"Felicia! You're riding! Yay!"

"How was it?"

"Great! I was trotting!"

"Get out! Already?"

"Yes."

"Are you going to ride with us now?"

"I want to."

"She did very well," said Francine, "but she's not ready

for that yet. A couple more lessons with me, and then she can ride with you."

Sophie admired Star. "Sweet horse."

Felicia placed her face against Star's, felt the warmth of the hairy jaw beneath her cheek. "Yes, she's sweet."

On the way home, Felicia tried to tell her mother what it was like to ride Star. "So awesome! Except now my bum's sore."

"Just remember to be careful."

CHAPTER 17
Flower

FLOWER STOOD on a chair and ran her fingers over the soft linen skirt. Mrs. Pemberton, her mouth brimming with pins, knelt in front of her to adjust the hem. The men sat at the table.

"This is a most complimentary letter of introduction, and written by a parson, a man of God." Noah Pemberton passed the folded letter back to her father.

"He took a shine to me, knew I wanted freedom and a better life for me and my family. He came to see us in our quarters, held a sort of church. It was good for us to be together, gave us a chance to talk. Master Chesley didn't mind."

"I think he minds now that you've gone away. Was your master unkind?"

"No...sometimes. He would beat those of us who dis-obeyed him, but he didn't torture anyone. He wasn't cruel, not like Samuel's master. And we had enough to eat."

"Yet you chose to take your family from that place."

"We were cared for, but we were still slaves. I wanted to earn money and buy our freedom, but he wouldn't hear of us leaving."

"I understand."

"I want to make my own way in this world. I know I can."

Flower felt very proud of her father as she listened to him speak, wanted to go and stand beside his chair, but Mrs. Pemberton asked her to turn around so she could adjust the other side of the skirt.

"Is Samuel your brother?" asked Noah.

"We met at the river. We helped each other as brothers would."

"The river has made Samuel's wound more trouble-some."

"He's ailing?"

"The doctor has been summoned."

Cleo appeared at the bottom of the stairs, the baby in her arms. "Husband," she said, interrupting their conversation.

"What is it, woman? We're meeting here."

"It's Gabriel. He's not nursing, and his body is very hot."

Eldon went immediately to the baby and felt his fore-head. Mrs. Pemberton stopped her work. The chair wobbled as she gripped it for support. Once on her feet, she lifted

Gabriel from his mother's arms and set him on the table, unwrapped his shawl, and frowned as she placed her ear against his chest, which rose and fell with each rapid breath. "I will prepare a poultice to lower his fever."

Flower sat by the fire and held her brother, while her frightened mother tore a clean sheet into pieces. Mrs. Pemberton smeared a paste on one of the rags and positioned it on the baby's laboring chest. Cleo then held him tight against her own.

Flower could see her mother's fear and absorbed it into herself. She wondered if they were being punished for leaving the master's household. Should they have stayed where they were and done what they were told? She wanted to ask these questions, but didn't; she knew such talk would make her mother even more anxious and her father angry.

Mrs. Pemberton's voice interrupted these thoughts. "Come child, I will show you how to help your wee brother." In her hand she held a cup of water and a spoon. Flower was shown how to place droplets of water gently on the baby's lips and into his mouth.

"That's right, just the smallest amount. We don't want him to choke."

Flower concentrated on her task, dripping liquid past Gabriel's dry, cracked lips. She could feel the heat pulsating from his body.

On the other side of the room, her father continued

his conversation with Mr. Pemberton. "We've always tried to be good people."

"Of that I have no doubt." Noah folded his hands and looked at Eldon. "I hate to say this, but you can't remain here. We are too close to the river. It is dangerous. Slave catchers are determined to recapture runaways and will travel great distances."

"Where should we go?"

"There are other places, other people. I cannot give you a map or list, but I will tell you, and you must commit this information to memory."

"How much time do we have here?"

"Two days."

A horse neighed in the distance. Flower shared a nervous glance with her father. Noah walked to the window, placed a comforting hand on Eldon's shoulder, and said, "Friends."

CHAPTER 18
Felicia

IT WAS LUNCHTIME in the cafeteria, and the four girls were in a huddle. Felicia nibbled a carrot stick and peered over Sophie's shoulder to glimpse the open pages of a gossip magazine.

"Do you think they'll stay married?"

"She's so gorgeous."

"*He's* so gorgeous!"

Josh interrupted. "Excuse me, ladies. Can we get this drama club meeting started?"

"Ladies?" Renate giggled.

"Whatever. We've only got this lunch hour before we get together with Mr. Butler. It's time to get serious."

"What about?"

"I've written a play."

"You have? What's it called?"

Josh shuffled some papers in his hands, looked around at the faces that now focused on him. "I haven't got a title for it yet. I'm still organizing a few ideas."

"Can you tell us about it? Like, what's the story?" Dodie asked.

"I've been reading some myths for inspiration, so it's set in ancient Greece. There are gods and goddesses, then these two main characters. I haven't decided on their names yet, maybe Zeus and Diana, I'm not sure. They fall in love but their families don't like each other. There's lots of action and then a big mix-up at the end. They wind up dead in each other's arms."

Sophie laughed. "Someone has already written a play like that. Ever heard of *Romeo and Juliet*?"

"This is totally different! It's about Greek gods, and there are battles!"

"So let's hear it."

Josh held the sheaf of papers against his chest. "It's not quite ready. It's a work in progress."

"I think we should do some stand-up comedy," said Matt.

"Easy for you. You're funny, but the rest of us aren't," said Dodie.

"I'll provide jokes. Coach you. Like, here's one: if a cat could talk...it wouldn't. See? Come on everybody. It'll be fun!"

"Excuse me. We were talking about my play."

"Boring," said Matt.

"We can make it interesting. I thought it could be

interactive. Everybody can contribute. The dialogue would be really realistic."

The students looked at each other and shrugged shoulders.

"I dunno."

"Maybe…"

A buzzer signaled the return to class. They started their migration down the hall. Josh walked beside Felicia. "I was thinking of you, Felicia, for a part in my play."

"Oh yeah?"

"Yeah. You could be Diana."

Felicia turned to Josh, open-mouthed with surprise. Josh's face immediately flamed red. He ducked his head and fled to the classroom.

Miss Peabody waited for them impatiently. "Come quickly and find your seats. The principal is going to make an important announcement to the whole school."

Mrs. Mackie's voice crackled through the speaker high in the corner of the classroom.

"Students, this year marks the one hundred and fiftieth birthday of the school, and we are going to celebrate this special occasion with the production of a play."

Felicia turned to look at Josh as Mrs. Mackie continued. "Mr. Butler has kindly offered to contribute his very own creation. I pass the microphone to Mr. Butler."

Mr. Butler's voice boomed into the room. "Hello,

students! What a pleasure it is for me to share my play with you all. I've called it *Happy Valley* in honor of our community, as well as the school. It's about our forebearers, the pioneers who came before us. Tryouts and casting will be next Monday in the cafeteria, then rehearsals start the following week. See you then!"

Josh's expression remained unchanged. Felicia admired his self-control. There wasn't a glimmer of the disappointment he had to be feeling. She started to write him a note.

Miss Peabody addressed her class. "Doesn't that sound exciting? I know I can hardly wait. In keeping with this pioneer theme, I am giving you an assignment." The collective groans did not dampen the teacher's enthusiasm. "I want you all to research your family history. Talk to your parents and all of your relatives. Find out what you can about those people in your past. Then, I want you to write a speech and create a visual display to present your findings to the class. The format may vary. I would like to see objects and hear stories from your family's past that can tell the class something about what life used to be like."

"How long does it have to be?" asked Renate.

"What if we find out something bad about our family, like we have a vampire uncle or something?" asked Matt.

"That is highly unlikely, Matthew."

"I dunno, my Uncle Bert has these weird teeth…"

There was a ripple of laughter. "Anyone else?" asked Miss Peabody.

Ashley's hand shot up. "My family, they were United Empire Loyalists!"

"Really? I'm sure we'll all be interested to hear about them."

Ashley continued, "I think there might have been some relative a long time ago that was from the royal family."

"We'll look forward to hearing your story."

Felicia sensed that Miss Peabody didn't believe Ashley. She watched as Ashley lowered her hand.

On the way home from school, the bus began to make grinding sounds. The driver pulled over to the side of the road and turned to the remaining riders.

"I don't like the sound of that—better not go any farther. I've got my cell phone if you want to call your parents to come and pick you up."

Some students went forward to call home, but the four girls decided to walk the rest of the way.

Felicia turned up her jacket collar to protect her neck and jammed her hands into her pockets. "Wow! It's cold!"

"We sometimes get these real cold spells even though it's not winter yet," said Renate.

"Not like the big city, eh?" added Sophie.

They began jogging to keep warm. Sophie's house

was the closest. She invited her friends to come in, but they decided to keep going. Renate's house was next. After Dodie and Felicia said good-bye to her, they put their heads down and walked quickly. The wind blew icy sleet against their faces.

"Maybe we should have stopped at Renate's and phoned home."

"Just a few more minutes."

Another gust of wind stopped them in their tracks, almost blowing their breath away.

"I'm freezing!"

"Let's go stand over there for a minute, beside those trees and out of the wind."

The two girls ran to the grove of trees. The large evergreens swayed and creaked, but they provided some protection from the early blast of winter.

"We'll stay here for a couple of minutes." Dodie jumped up and down on the spot. "This helps to keep the circulation going. Wiggle your toes. That helps."

"Look! We can see our breath!" They puffed and laughed at the clouds of moisture coming out of their mouths. "Your cheeks are all red," said Felicia.

"So's your nose!"

They stood shivering together, preparing to go out again into the storm.

"Did you hear that?"

"What?"

"Listen!"

It was barely audible, the softest cry.

"Yeah! Where's it coming from?" They looked around them, and then Felicia pointed to a large tree. There was an opening at the base, and something was huddled inside it. They knelt down to get a better view. Felicia hesitated, but then reached in and extracted a tiny sodden bundle.

"Oh my gosh! It's a baby kitten!"

"Hiding in there, trying to keep warm."

"The poor thing!"

"I wonder where its mother is."

"I don't think it has a mother right now."

"What'll we do? Can you take it home, Dodie?"

"No, I can't. My brother has asthma—and a jillion allergies. Better put it back."

Felicia started to return the animal to its hiding place. It felt like a bundle of twigs in her hands. "I can feel its ribs."

"It's probably starving."

"Maybe we can take it to the Humane Society."

"You'll have to take it home first. Can you do that?"

"My mom will freak."

"Does she hate cats?"

"No."

"Take it home then, and give it something to eat. A

vet should see it. You can call the animal protection people tomorrow."

Felicia hesitated, then placed the kitten inside her jacket. It didn't scratch, just settled in. The girls walked out from of the shelter of the trees and put their heads down, against the wind. As she struggled home, Felicia felt the warmth of the kitten, damp against her chest, and wondered if a cat was able to understand the concept of gratitude.

CHAPTER 19
Flower

GENTLE HANDS palpated Gabriel's chest and neck. "Poor wee babe, too young to be swimming in a cold river." The doctor laid his ear against the rapidly moving chest and listened. "What care has he been given?"

Sarah Pemberton described the poultice. Dr. Simon placed two fingers on Gabriel's neck. "Is he drinking?"

"His sister has been giving him water."

Doctor Simon looked at Flower, noticing her for the first time.

"You've been giving water to your brother?"

"Yes, Sir."

"And how did you do that?"

"Mrs. Pemberton showed me how to drop water from a spoon into Gabriel's mouth, just the tiniest bit."

"Did he swallow or choke?"

"Most spilled from his mouth, no choking."

"You did well, a good help to your sick brother. Now, who else ails in this household?" Noah Pemberton led Dr.

Simon up the stairs.

After Samuel had been examined, the two men returned to the kitchen, their faces grim. They sat at the table with Eldon as Mrs. Pemberton and the doctor's wife served tea and biscuits. Flower and her mother stayed by the warmth of the hearth. Cleo held her baby close as Flower aimed at his mouth with a spoon, tipping in drops of water.

"Has this other person been badly treated?" asked Mrs. Simon, as she and her hostess settled in chairs.

"His right ear was severed from his head, and the wound is now festering."

Mrs. Simon brought her hand to her mouth. She turned to Sarah Pemberton. The women shook their heads and looked down into their teacups.

"The institution of slavery is an abomination," Dr. Simon said. "Men forget how to be human." He turned to Eldon. "Are you in good health, at least?"

"Yes, I'm strong, and my tiredness is lifting."

Mrs. Pemberton passed the plate of biscuits to Eldon. "Take. Eat. I know you're hungry." She stood up from the table and carried the biscuits to Cleo and Flower.

"We must make plans," said Noah.

"Samuel should stay with us," said Dr. Simon. I'll be able to look after him until his wound has started to heal and he's well enough to travel." He looked toward his wife, who nodded in agreement.

"We have, at the most, two days' grace. Then the jackals will be howling."

"When the babe can nurse again, he will be healthy enough to move."

"The family would be well suited at the Jensons'. Jeremiah Jenson is unwell. Eldon would be most helpful there."

"What is your plan?" Dr. Simon asked Eldon.

"I led my family through the hills and across the river. Now we must make our way to a place called Ripley."

Noah said, "Tell us about this pastor who visited you, the man who wrote the letter to introduce you."

"He started coming to see us on Sunday afternoons," Eldon began. "We sang hymns. He told stories from the Bible, stories about brave people: Daniel in the lion's den, David and Goliath, Jonah in the whale."

"Was your master happy with that?"

"I don't know. I'm not sure. The Reverend stopped coming for a bit, and then one Sunday he showed up again. He talked about heaven. Someone told him we didn't know about heaven but we sure knew about hell."

Everyone's eyes fell on Eldon's clasped hands. He continued, "One afternoon he spoke to three of us after the service. He told us about a real promised land, a place where we could be free. He told us a bit about how to get there, said we would have a friend in Ripley who would tell us how to get to Canada."

Dr. Simon turned to Noah Pemberton. "He'll need time to memorize more information."

Flower listened to the hum of talk on the other side of the room. Her mother was asleep, her head slanted toward her shoulder. Flower concentrated on the drops of water pooling inside Gabriel's open mouth. She set the spoon down and rubbed his downy cheek with her knuckle. He frowned and swallowed.

"Gabriel?"

CHAPTER 20
Felicia

FELICIA BURST through the front door, stood in the hallway, and started to unwind her scarf from around her neck. Delia jumped up from her chair in the living room.

"Look at you! Take off those wet clothes before you catch your death. I'll run a warm bath." She used the tail end of the scarf to pat Felicia's face dry and started to unbutton Felicia's jacket as she spoke. A wet, skeletal kitten face peeked out at her. Delia drew back in alarm. "What on earth…?"

"Mom, I found this poor baby cat…"

"Oh no!"

"Stranded in the storm…"

"We can't keep it!"

"It doesn't have a mom…"

"No way."

"Look! It's starving."

Florence stood in the kitchen doorway. "Felicia, you're home—thank heavens! What's all the fuss about?"

"She's brought in some filthy little animal," said Delia.

Florence walked into the hall. "Let's see."

"It's just a baby, Nana."

"Covered in germs," said Delia. "Probably has rabies."

Felicia held the kitten in her hands so that her grandmother could see it. It blinked in the sudden light. It tried to meow but had no voice. "Dodie said I should give it some food and take it to the vet."

Delia looked at it and shook her head. "And who's going to pay for that?"

"Does that cost a lot?" asked Felicia. She hoped it didn't.

"We'll find something for it." Florence started back to the kitchen.

"First a horse and now a cat," Delia said. "What else will you come up with? An elephant?"

Felicia kicked off her wet shoes and slithered out of her jacket as she held onto the damp bundle of kitten. Her mother stripped off wet socks as Felicia stood on one foot and then the other. "You need a bath. Your skin is icy cold."

"I'll be up in a minute." Felicia headed into the kitchen. "Should we warm the milk, Nana?"

"That's just what I'm doing. I'm not sure cow's milk is the best thing for a kitten, but it's all I can think of at the moment. Put the kitten in that cardboard box and wrap a towel around it. It'll be just fine while you have your bath."

Felicia raced up the stairs, stripped off her wet clothes, and stepped into the tub. Delia had added bath salts. Felicia meant to jump in and jump out, but once she settled in the warm, scented water, the sheer delight of it, after her frigid journey, kept her there. She leaned back and let the water soothe and warm her.

When Felicia returned to the kitchen, Florence was washing a turkey baster.

"What's that for?" asked Felicia.

"It might be useful for giving the milk. We'll try it. Wrap that kitten in the towel. It's still shivering."

Delia sat at the table sipping a mug of tea. "I can't believe we're doing all this for a stray animal that's probably carrying a horrible disease."

"Did you ever have a pet, Mom?"

"No, never. This is a new experience." Delia looked at her mother.

"I used to feed the odd stray," said Florence, "but I never let anything in the house." She approached her granddaughter, now holding the toweled kitten in her lap. "See if it will take some milk from this." Florence extended the plastic baster full of milk. The kitten sniffed it, then opened its mouth and began to drink.

"It's sucking on it, like a baby!"

"What are we going to do when the other end works?" asked Delia.

"We'll tear up some newspaper and put it in the box, see if it uses that."

"It has to stay in the kitchen," said Delia.

Felicia was entranced with the feeding. "This really works, Nana. I knew it was starving." She stroked the tiny, bony head with a finger. "Feeling better now, baby?"

Later, the family sat over supper. "Do you have any homework?" asked Delia.

"There's a special project I have to do for school. Maybe you both can help me. There's going to be a big celebration with a play and everything, 'cause the school is one hundred and fifty years old this year."

"Really?"

"And Miss Peabody has asked everybody in our class to find out about their families, from way back, and then write it up and present it to the class."

Delia and Florence exchanged a glance. "Mmm hmm."

"So tell me all about my family. I hope there's somebody interesting. Matt thinks his uncle might have been a vampire."

Florence said, "I'm pretty sure we didn't have any vampires. My great-grandfather was a cabinet maker."

"A what maker?"

"A cabinet maker—sort of like a fancy carpenter. He made fine furniture."

"Okay. I guess I should write that down. Hold on." Felicia returned to the table with pen and pad. "Who else?"

"My father worked on the railroad as a porter," Florence said.

"Tell me again about my dad. I love hearing about him. He worked in a bank, right?"

"Yes. He was very good with numbers," Delia said. "Had a mind like a steel trap when it came to figuring things out."

"And he liked music, too."

"Yes, he strummed a guitar from time to time."

"And?"

"And he loved to read books. He read to you all the time when you were little."

"He was so young when he died."

"Yes, only forty-two. The leukemia got him." Florence reached over and squeezed Delia's hand.

"Are you going to write about me, too?" Delia asked.

"I'll say you're a career woman, Mom."

Delia's sad expression dissolved as she threw her head back and laughed. "That's a good one! I'm a secretary at a car dealership."

"An administrative assistant, remember? Any other interesting women?"

"Let me think," said Florence. "Of course, there's your great-aunt Agnes. She painted beautifully, just like you do. I

94

have one of her paintings in my bedroom."

"The picture of the bowl of fruit on a table?"

"That's the one."

"Okay, Aunt Agnes the artist. Maybe I can take that painting to school and show everyone."

"I'm not sure about that. I'll think about it. Oh, and there's a family Bible with all kinds of names listed at the front. It belonged to my mother."

"What did your mother do?"

"Raised seven children, that's what she did."

Felicia imagined having six siblings. She had dim memories of her grandmother's large family, their past get-togethers, tables laden with food and drink, the din of many conversations punctuated by laughter, singing, music. "Didn't someone play the piano?"

"My sisters, Evelyn and Julia. They were very talented. I think Julia even composed some music. There should be a song sheet somewhere; it used to be kept in the piano bench."

Felicia continued to make notes. "Anybody related to the royal family?" she asked, pen poised above her list.

"Now, there's a silly question!"

"One of the girls in my class said she thought someone from her family was related to some royalty."

"Oh?"

"Do you think she might be lying?"

"Maybe."

"Why would she lie about her family?"

"Maybe she's stretching the truth, or it's just wishful thinking."

"Was there anyone really special in our family?"

"Everyone was special."

"You know what I mean—really good or really bad."

"We were all pretty good," said Florence, "my family."

"That's the truth," agreed Delia.

"I wonder if someone from way back in our family liked to ride horses, like I do."

"Perhaps, but I think their horses were used for work back then, not pleasure."

Felicia closed her eyes and imagined riding long ago. Her billowy skirt would make it hard to sit up on the saddle. Maybe she'd drive a carriage. She'd sit up on a special seat, long reins in hand. The horse would respond to her gentle tug, and they would set off on a pleasant journey, trotting along a sun-dappled lane.

"How about way back in the olden days?" Felicia's pen hovered over the pad.

"Some of that information just disappeared over the years," said Florence, "but we do have some things in that old trunk I have. I know my grandmother's grandparents came up from Virginia before the Civil War."

"How did they get here? Maybe they rode horses."

"I doubt it. They would have been on the run, and it's unlikely they could afford a horse, unless someone gave them one."

"What were they on the run from?"

"From slavery, sweetie."

"How would they know where to run to?"

"They probably received some help. There was a system of helpers called the 'Underground Railroad.'"

"They took a train?"

"The Underground Railroad was a kind of secret network of people helping other people escape slavery and come north to Canada, where they could be free," Florence explained.

"I hope someone gave them a horse so they didn't have to walk. It must have been hard," said Felicia. "Just imagine."

"Yes," said Delia, "just imagine."

CHAPTER 21
Flower

FLOWER STOOD with her parents as they said good-bye to the Pembertons. Gabriel peeked over his mother's shoulder at everyone. A rectangular wooden wagon with one harnessed horse waited in the drive. Cleo said to their protectors, "Thank you for all your kindness."

"We are only doing our duty…what we believe is right. Go in safety and help others like yourselves."

When the family was settled in the wagon, the driver clucked and slapped a rein. The horse responded, pulling it forward with a lurch. Flower watched as the Pembertons slowly receded into the distance, then turned and aligned herself against her mother's side. Samuel lay behind them on a pallet of hay. He moaned at each bump in the road.

Within two hours they reached the Simons' and were welcomed by the doctor's wife. "Come in, all of you, and rest a while. I've prepared a small lunch."

They followed her into the kitchen, except for Samuel, who was led into a separate room so the doctor could attend to his wound. Flower stood at the kitchen window, watched as the driver filled a pail of water for his horse. He chatted with the animal, stroked its side as it sucked up the liquid, and then placed a handful of hay on the ground at its feet.

Mrs. Simon looked up as the driver entered the kitchen. "There's a pump in the yard for washing up." He bowed his head, his dusty hat clutched in both hands, and made an abrupt turn. When he came back into the room, he spread his hands out for her to see, like a small boy.

"That's better. We love our horses, but they carry dirt best left outdoors." She ladled steaming soup into bowls as she spoke. Flower carried them to the table. A jug of water and a basket of biscuits sat in the center. They sat down and, after Dr. Simon said grace, ate their lunch. Samuel spooned the soup into his mouth with a shaky hand.

"A good, quiet day for travel," the doctor commented.

"The roads are dry," offered the driver.

"After all that rain!"

"Yes."

"The babe is well?" asked Dr. Simon.

Gabriel sat in his mother's lap and sucked on a spoon. He suddenly sneezed, and as Cleo tidied him with the edge of her shawl, he waved clenched fists in protest, dropped the spoon, and began to cry.

"He's fretful," said Cleo.

"But nursing?"

"Yes, better."

"Good. I will give you a paregoric for the journey," said Dr. Simon.

"Medicine?"

"It's a special medicine. It won't hurt him, but it will make him sleepy. If he cries and people hear him, you could be caught. We don't want that to happen."

After lunch, they prepared to leave. Still not well enough to travel any farther, Samuel lay in bed. The family stood by it to say their farewells. Flower watched as he and her father clasped hands.

"Till we meet again."

Flower stepped forward and extended her own hand. Samuel looked abandoned and forlorn, with the bandage looped over where his ear used to be and under his chin. She wanted to say something encouraging to him, that they would soon reunite in a free place. She paused and thought, then said, "I hope you get better soon."

He tried to smile at her, but his mouth gave up right away.

"Courage, brother," said Eldon.

They left his bedside and gathered at the front of the house where a horse and wagon waited for them. The driver directed the family to the back of his rig, then lifted a blanket and the lid of a large box. "When we reach a certain place, you must ride in here, out of sight. I'll tell you when."

As the family climbed aboard, Doctor Simon placed a small vial of liquid in Cleo's lap. "Just a drop should be enough."

"Good-bye and thank you."

"Safe journey."

The wagon swayed forward as they set off down the road. The horse trotted for a distance, then settled into a steady walk. Flower sat dreamily, looked at the stony roadside, the trees with leaves drying to shades of reds and yellows. After a while they came to a bend in the road.

The driver pulled back on the reins and said, "It's time."

The space wasn't large. The four of them lay side by side, Flower and Gabriel in the middle. Cleo placed a drop of the medication on her finger and then put the finger into the baby's mouth. He squeezed his eyes shut in disgust and began to whimper. The box top thudded down in place. An explosion of dust caused them to sneeze, then Eldon said "shhh," and they were silent.

The wagon started to move again. Flower felt close to the road—heard the creak of rotating wooden wheels, the ping of stone, the grind of dirt, even the snorting breath of the laboring horse as he drew his load forward.

The first voice shocked her.

"Good day."

"G'day."

The motion continued, sounds intensified: people, animals, and other wagons. They came to an abrupt stop, and reins were tied in place. Flower heard the driver leap down to the ground. Someone walked by. Flower's heart began to pound so hard she thought surely everyone could hear it and they would be discovered. Her father found her hand and squeezed it. Gabriel slept on, his breath warm against her face.

The driver returned, another man with him.

"That rain yesterday…the street was a sea of mud."

"The roads are dry today."

"Easier going."

There was the sudden scrape of the box lid. Flower held her breath and clamped her eyes shut.

"No, leave that be!" The driver's sharp command kept them hidden. "That bit's for the Jensons! We'll put the rest on top."

Six things were thrown into the back of the cart, landing with thumps above them. The air was dusty again. Eldon's hand covered his daughter's face, and Cleo clasped her baby close to her.

"Next thing we know, it'll be snowing."

"That's the truth."

"How's Jenson? Hear he's poorly."

"I'll find out soon enough."

The driver climbed up onto his seat and picked up the

reins. "I'll be off then." He clucked his command to the horse, and the wagon moved forward. The family stayed silent even after they left the town and were again on country roads. Flower fell asleep.

She woke up as the wagon jolted to a stop. The driver lifted off the supplies and then the box lid. "We're here."

CHAPTER 22
Felicia

FELICIA ARRIVED at the tryouts just as Mr. Butler bustled in, carrying a large folder under his arm. She watched as he placed it on the table with a dramatic flourish. "Welcome, everyone! I hope you're feeling creative."

Questions rang out. "What's the play about?"

"Are you giving out copies?"

Mr. Butler raised his hands. "Just give me a minute and I'll tell you. I have written a play about the pioneers who came to this area. There are six main characters and twenty secondary ones. I have copies available for those who would like to audition."

"Is the play complete, or do we have a chance to work on dialogue, say—"

Josh was interrupted before he finished his question. "It stays as it's written. I don't want any changes."

"Does it have any funny bits?" asked Matt.

"No. This is a serious subject."

Matt turned to the group of drama club students and

crossed his eyes. Josh doodled on a piece of paper.

Mr. Butler lifted a script out of the folder, pushed his glasses farther up on his nose, and began to read. "There once was a time when the timber was high, and all of the trees grew straight up to the sky..." His voice rose and dipped with emotive intensity, despite the undercurrent of sighs and shuffling feet. Three loud sneezes interrupted the flow of words. The teacher pulled a tissue from his pocket and blew his nose.

"How long does this take, Mr. Butler?"

"Can you give out copies now?"

"Is there any music in this?"

"Yes. There are several songs, and there will be a pianist who will accompany them. All cast members will do some singing, and, by the way, I need four singing pioneers. You'll only have about twelve speaking lines, not much to memorize."

"What do you think?" Dodie whispered to the others.

"Okay," said Felicia. Renate and Sophie nodded.

Dodie spoke up. "Excuse us, Mr. Butler, there are four of us here and we can sing."

"Yes? Good. Come up on the stage. Let's hear you."

Felicia felt fine until she stood in the center of the stage and looked out at the sloping seats of the auditorium, curious students now staring in her direction. "What are we going to sing?" she asked Dodie.

"Girls? Anytime," said Mr. Butler.

Dodie took charge. "We'll sing what we sang before riding yesterday. Turn around and face the audience. We'll each do a verse. I'll go first, then Renate, then Sophie, then Felicia. We'll all sing the chorus." They looked out to the back of the vast room and took deep breaths. Dodie muttered "here goes" and began to sing. Her voice was clear and controlled. Three voices joined her in the chorus. Renate sang the next verse, their voices melded in the chorus, and then it was Sophie's turn. She was shy but brave, and her voice quavered only a little at the beginning. Finally, Felicia sang out, surprising herself with the pure pleasure of performing. They swayed with a shared rhythm at the end. Their audience stood up and moved along with them. After the girls finished, they were rewarded with whistles and cheers and wild applause. The girls clapped back to the students, laughing and hugging each other.

"Very nice," said Mr. Butler, his voice barely audible over the din. "Yes, very nice, thank you."

The girls made their way back to their seats, feeling happy and accomplished.

Josh leaned forward from behind Felicia and patted her on her shoulder. "You were amazing."

"Such talent," said Matt, "here in our little burg."

Mr. Butler took charge once more. "We have quite a few readings, so let's get started. I need six First Nations people. Who's interested?" Three hands were raised. "That's three, how about another three?"

"How about we skip this?" whispered Dodie. "We have our parts and the clock's ticking. If we hurry, we can still fit in our riding class."

The girls stood up and made their way out.

"Leaving?" asked Josh.

"We've got to go riding," explained Felicia.

"I'll call you later and tell you what happened," said Josh.

"Thanks."

"Giving up already?" Ashley had her legs stretched out so each girl had to make her way over them.

"We've got things to do," said Renate, as she stepped on Ashley's left foot. "Bye!"

CHAPTER 23
Flower

FLOWER AND her family climbed out of their hiding place and stepped down off the wagon. Before them was a wooden-frame farmhouse, weathered and worn. A thin woman who looked as weather-beaten as her house stood on the covered verandah. She held a baby in her arms and was surrounded by four children. The tallest was a girl who brushed unruly hair from her eyes and stared at Flower.

Eldon and the driver unloaded supplies from the wagon. They were directed by Mrs. Jenson to carry them to a shed. No one said anything until the men came back and the driver asked about Mr. Jenson.

"You can see him if you like. His days are long and hard. He needs the talk of another man," said his wife. She turned to Eldon and his family. "I'll show you your place." She led them to the barn, the children following behind her like ducklings. The barn was large, with an open area in the center and stalls on each side. A ladder led to a hayloft. One of the boys ran ahead and started to climb it.

"Get down from there before you break your neck! That's just what I need, another one lame."

The boy skittered down the ladder and stood again with his siblings. Flower watched his efforts with fascination and then turned her gaze to include the other children, only to discover they were all staring at her, even the baby in its mother's arms.

Mrs. Jenson continued, "There's some hay to sleep on, and the animals can come in if you need more warmth."

"Thank you, Missus," said Cleo.

All was quiet again as Mrs. Jenson appeared to organize her thoughts. Finally she said, "You'll be wanting some nourishment."

"That would be most kind," said Cleo.

"Much appreciated," said Eldon.

They started back toward the house, the wind blowing dust up around their feet. The adventurous boy led the way, but stopped at the door to let his mother enter first. The interior of the house was sparse, not at all like the Pembertons'. In the center stood a rectangular table with benches on either side. A rocking chair sat by a black woodstove, and in the corner was a cot, the driver standing beside it. The children scurried to sit on the benches, except for the eldest girl, who took the baby from her mother's arms and settled in the rocking chair.

"I'll make some tea, then," said Mrs. Jenson. She

placed the kettle on the stove and brought mugs to the table. "Here now," she addressed her children, "make room for everyone." She gestured to Eldon, Cleo, and Flower, who watched space being made for them, then sat down.

"How's about yourself? Will you be wanting some tea as well?"

A voice from the cot, raspy and weak, answered, "I'll try some."

The driver said, "A nice cup of tea—just the thing to perk us all up." He walked to the table and sat down.

Mrs. Jenson poured tea. No biscuits were served. She brought a mug to her husband, helped him raise himself onto one elbow, and then held the mug close to his mouth so he could sip it. When he had had enough, he flopped back down with a sigh, and she came back to the table.

"Hettie, come and have some tea."

The girl left the rocking chair, placed the baby back in Mrs. Jenson's lap, and sat down beside Flower. No one spoke; the only sounds were the swallows of tea from mugs and the wind outside. Cleo unwrapped Gabriel from his sling. He sat up in her lap, spied a spoon, and reached for it. Successful, he stuck it in his mouth and surveyed the group around the table, his gaze stopping at the Jenson infant. Both babies regarded each other with solemn expressions until Gabriel waved the spoon in the air and made a joyful cry. The other baby laughed. His mother offered him a spoon.

Cleo said, "What handsome children you have."

A glimmer of a smile played on Mrs. Jenson's lips. She could not conceal her pride in her brood. "That is the truth."

"Many helpful hands."

Mrs. Jenson's face became downcast once more. "Not enough help for all that needs doing, I'm afraid."

"We are able to help, not just hide," said Eldon.

Mrs. Jenson looked across the table at him. Her glance was shy but appraising. "You look strong enough."

"That I am."

"You must speak to my husband."

Flower's father got up from the table and, within two paces, stood at the makeshift bedside. "I'm sorry for your trouble." He stood tall and straight, towering over the slight figure beneath the blanket.

"Yes. I've come to a sad pass."

"Tell me what needs doing."

"The harvest is still in the fields and on the trees, waiting to rot. Tools are getting rusty, fences falling down."

"I'll be glad to make things right in exchange for a safe refuge for myself and my family."

"Agreed."

"No one comes to help you? Do your neighbors drop by?"

"We have no neighbors to speak of. The missus goes to town occasionally for supplies. She can manage that."

Mrs. Jenson spoke up. "Children, outside now!" She handed the baby again to Hettie, so Cleo passed Gabriel into Flower's outstretched arms.

Hettie led the way to the porch. She and Flower sat down on the top step with both babies facing each other. The boys settled at their feet.

"Sing us a song, Hettie," one of the brothers commanded.

"Give me a minute." Hettie readjusted the squirming infant in her lap, then sat and studied Gabriel and Flower. "Your skin is brown," she said.

Flower, in turn, regarded Hettie and her family. She had never seen such pale people. Their hair was yellowy white, their eyes light gray, and their skin seemed almost transparent, spattered with tiny tan spots across their noses. "You all have hardly any color."

"Sometimes the sun burns us red, but then it goes away."

"Does that hurt?"

"A little. What's your baby's name?"

"Gabriel."

"Like the angel in the Bible?"

"The very one. And he is a little angel, aren't you?" She gave Gabriel a hug, and he snuggled against her. "What are the names of your kin?"

The boy who had climbed the ladder spoke up. "She's

Hettie. I'm Wilfred. This here's Edgar, then Joseph, and the babe's George."

"Georgie," said Hettie, giving her baby a squeeze. "I'm the only girl."

"Do you look after everybody?" asked Flower.

Wilfred stood up. "I don't need anyone to look after me."

"What's your name?" asked Hettie.

"Flower."

"Oh, that is the prettiest name I ever heard."

"Thank you."

"How did you get to be here?"

Flower told them of her family's long walk, the creation of the raft, and the dangerous river crossing. "Gabriel was ailing, but now he's better."

"Our Pa is sick. He cut his leg real bad taking down a tree. Now he sleeps a lot and nothing much gets done."

"Hettie!" Mrs. Jenson's anxious face appeared in the doorway. "Here's the slate. Do some sums with the boys."

Joseph took the square from his mother and handed it to Hettie. Georgie was transferred to Flower's lap, as the boys gathered round their sister. Numbers were scraped on the slate, and the boys took turns giving the answers. Flower coped with the babies and tried to follow what they were doing. The door creaked open again, and her father stood on the porch. He watched the activity with approval and then said, "I need a good strong boy to help me hitch up the horse."

Wilfred jumped up. "I can do that."

"Come along then." Eldon gave both of his children a pat on the head and then strode to the barn. Wilfred ran ahead.

CHAPTER 24
Felicia

FELICIA RETRIEVED the homework from her backpack. The phone jingled just as she opened a book.

"Hey Felicia." It was Josh. He cleared his throat and his voice accidentally squeaked. "How are you doing?"

"Fine."

"What's new?"

"Not much. How about you?"

"I'm okay. What did you think of the meeting?"

"The four of us singing was exciting. What happened at the end? Was the last bit interesting, the part I missed?"

"People were assigned roles. I'm going to play the lead, Mayor Thomas."

"That's great!"

"Except guess who's playing the lead lady?"

"Who?"

"Ashley! The snob goddess!"

"Is that okay with you?"

"Not really, but it's too late for me to do anything about it."

"I guess."

"There's more."

"Yeah?"

"Mr. Butler switched you from your part to one of the Native people. Cynthia is going to be one of the four singing pioneers with Dodie, Renate, and Sophie."

"Oh no!"

"I know."

Felicia felt her face getting hot. "Why would he go and do that?" Delia appeared in the kitchen doorway and made the "time" signal with her hands. "Do you know what, Josh? I got home late, and I only just started my homework a few minutes ago. I have to go now."

"Oh, okay." Josh sounded disappointed. "See you tomorrow."

Felicia bent over her assignment once more. Satisfied, Delia left the kitchen. After filling one page with answers, Felicia put down her pencil and silently slipped across the room to peer into the box. The kitten was sound asleep, curled in a circle.

The phone rang again. Felicia snatched the receiver from its cradle on the wall.

It was Dodie. "How's the kitten?"

"Unbelievably cute."

"Is your mom upset?"

"A little." Felicia was tempted to say, "Guess what? Josh just called me," but she didn't. "You'll never believe what I just found out. Mr. Butler cast Cynthia as the fourth singing pioneer, not me!"

"You're kidding! That's gross."

"I know." Delia reappeared in the kitchen, glowering and pointing at her watch. "I've gotta go. I'll tell you all about it tomorrow at lunch."

Felicia hung up and said to her mother, "I can't believe the way you behave sometimes. It's embarrassing."

"The way I behave."

"Yes. You behave so rudely."

"I'm rude."

"Yes. How would you like it if I interrupted you when you were talking to a friend on the phone? I think you'd hate it. It's rude and pushy."

"If I didn't push a little, you wouldn't get anything done."

"I get lots done. I don't need you to push me."

"Well, I'll leave you now to do your homework— *unpushed*."

"Thank you. Now, Nana," Felicia called out to her grandmother, "where did you say that Bible was?"

"Upstairs, dear, in the old trunk in the bottom of my bedroom cupboard. There's a special box in there, too, with things that might be useful."

Felicia came down, carrying the box atop the Bible. "Here they are."

She presented them to Florence, who was sitting at the kitchen table. Felicia looked at the large book. It was heavy, with thick, dark covers. The words "Family Bible" were raised in dark red with gold edges. She started to turn the pages. A few photographs spilled out. They were sepia-toned pictures of women wearing formal taffetas and men in high collars and floppy bow ties, all with solemn faces.

"These people look pretty serious. Do you know who they are?"

"There should be names on the back," Florence said, turning over one of the photos.

Felicia picked up a small bundle of faded flowers. "Did you wear these to a dance, Nana?"

"Yes, dear, pinned at my waist. It's called a corsage."

"What was your dress like?"

"Periwinkle blue taffeta with embroidery on the bodice."

"And a long skirt?"

"Oh yes, with petticoats and crinolines beneath."

"That swirled out when you danced?"

Florence smiled at the memory and nodded.

"Cool."

Felicia picked up a typewritten card that had an official look to it. "What's this?"

"Your great-grandfather's union card. He was a steward." Felicia ran her hand over all the items, then picked up a medal fastened to a striped ribbon. "Is this from a war?"

"My great-uncle Charlie," said Florence. "A sergeant in the army. He never came home."

"How am I going to attach some of this stuff to the board?"

"Oh, my dear," said Florence, "you can't take any of these things to school."

"What! What am I going to do then?"

"Write the stories Nana's been telling you about," said Delia.

"I have been writing, but it's not enough! I can't just read off a paper, I'll lose marks. Miss Peabody said we had to bring something in to show. All the other kids are bringing stuff in."

"These are precious things of your Nana's."

"That's it. I'm going to fail!"

"I think it's time for some hot chocolate," said Delia. She pulled three mugs from the cupboard, filled them with milk and a dollop of chocolate sauce, and popped them into the microwave. "Where are those paints of yours?"

"What paints?"

"You know very well what paints. Your paints upstairs in the closet."

"I haven't done any painting for ages. And why would I paint now?"

"You can paint these heirlooms and stories so you'll have something to show to the class."

The microwave pinged and Delia removed the mugs, then took a sip of hers. "Just right!"

Felicia raised her head from the table, dragged her feet up the stairs, and returned with a sheet of Bristol board and her paint box and brushes. She remained sulky as she sipped her drink. "I guess I'll need some magazines and newspaper, and glue and scissors. Nana, do you have any fancy material?"

"I think I can find some."

Felicia picked up a brush.

CHAPTER 25
Flower

FLOWER WATCHED as her father slid a stone against the blade of a long, curved knife. Satisfied, he ran a finger along an edge and whistled. "That should do it."

"What's that for, Pa?" The scythe glinted in the morning sun, sharp and dangerous. She didn't want him to touch it.

"There's still some hay to cut, to neaten things."

"You might hurt yourself, like Hettie's Pa."

"I have no plan for doing that."

"You've done a lot of good work here."

"Yes."

"Are you finished?"

"I'd like to be. We need to be moving on. They tell me it's a long way to Ripley. I don't like us staying in one place too long like this."

"Can we leave once you've done everything?" Flower watched as Wilfred made his way toward them.

"We'll be leaving soon."

"I want to help you."

"You help the elder girl with the children and the women with the house. That's what you should do."

"Women's work for you and men's work for me! Isn't that so, Eldon?" said Wilfred as he joined them.

"Seems to be the way of the world. Now, get yourself a rake, young man, and follow me."

Flower watched her father walk away with Wilfred, and she envied their male companionship. They did things together that seemed to be enjoyable as well as important.

She returned to the house to find Hettie sitting on the bottom porch step, tracing letters in the dirt with her finger.

"Can you read?" asked Hettie.

"I wasn't allowed to go to school. Maybe when we get to the place where we're free, I'll be able to learn. I hope so."

"Do you know any letters at all?"

"Not yet."

"Look," said Hettie. "I can sign my name."

She carefully drew the letters in the dirt.

"Let me try," said Flower. They both laughed as she outlined the image of a flower. "Do you have any books?"

"We have a Bible. I don't think Ma will let me touch it. It's for good."

"Hettie!"

"Yes, Ma."

"What are you two lazy girls up to when there's these boys need looking after? Come in here and help with the lunch."

After their meal the others trooped off to help in the fields, leaving Flower in the cabin with a heavy baby in each arm. They wriggled impatiently; when she set them down, they fought over the spoons placed in their fists. She decided to use the spoons like puppets and improvised a story.

"Aren't you the clever one."

The sudden intrusion of a croaky voice made her jump. "Excuse me?"

"With the babes, settling their disagreement with a little theater. Leave them for a moment and come here."

Flower's instinct was to avoid the dark corner. Reluctantly, she approached the cot. Mr. Jenson was even more pale than his children. Hair stood up in spikes on his head, his chin was bristly, and there was a whiff of sickness about him.

"The babes are fine for the time being. I could use a sip of water."

Flower pumped some water into a mug. Mr. Jenson hoisted himself up onto one elbow and drank quickly. "I shouldn't be thirsty. I've been doing nothing at all." He sighed and lay down again. "What's your name, then? Tell me about yourself. I could use a good story. I've got nothing in my mind but worry."

She told him the tale of her family on the run. He listened with interest, nodding and frowning at different parts of her account.

When the babies began to cry and rub their eyes, Flower placed them side by side in the cradle and rocked them to sleep.

Mr. Jenson started to speak again. "What's it like outside?"

Flower followed his glance to the window. "It's cooler."

"No sign of rain?"

"No. I can't see any clouds."

"Sometimes I can smell the rain coming."

"You can?"

"Yes. And I love the smell of the earth after a rain, everything nourished."

Flower ran her finger along the edge of the cradle. It was dusty.

Mr. Jenson continued. "Oh, how I'd love to be outside, seeing the earth, smelling it, working with it."

"Would you like some tea?"

"Thank you. That might perk me up."

Flower was pumping water into the kettle when Wilfred burst through the door, his siblings close behind him. He managed to make his voice heard above the sudden din of adult voices and the cries of wakened babies. "Look! It's Dr. Simon in his carriage, coming fast up the road!"

CHAPTER 26
Felicia

"COMING to lunch?" Sophie asked.

"I have a chore to do," answered Felicia. "I'll meet you in the cafeteria in a few minutes."

Felicia walked purposefully down the hall. She stopped in front of Mr. Butler's classroom and took a deep breath, then poked her head around the doorframe. He stopped reading when he noticed her. They both said hello.

"Mr. Butler, I want to talk to you for a minute about the play."

"Of course. What is it?"

"Didn't you like my singing?"

"Yes. It was very good."

"Then why did you give that part to Cynthia?"

"I thought the other part would be perfect for you."

"Why did you think that?"

"Well, I just thought it would suit you better. I thought you might be more comfortable in that role. What if I made you a Native princess? Would you like that?"

"Mr. Butler, I auditioned. You gave me the part of the pioneer because I was good. I want to be a singing pioneer with my friends. It's not fair what you're doing."

"All right, Felicia, I didn't know you felt so strongly about it. You can be one of the pioneers."

Felicia's "thank you" was a little breathless. She was glad to leave Mr. Butler's presence before he could see that she was nervous, not calm and logical as she had wanted to appear. Resentment at having to make such an effort was followed by relief. She had stood up for herself, and she'd made him change his mind.

Felicia decided she had time to go to the library before meeting her friends for lunch. Mr. Allenby sat behind the broad desk just inside the entrance. "What can I do for you today, young lady?"

"I want to do some research," said Felicia.

"Oh yes, in what field?"

"History."

"Following up on some local lore, are you, stimulated by Mr. Butler's extravaganza?"

"Sort of."

Mr. Allenby got to his feet and walked to the bookshelves. "Lots of interesting stuff here; there's the Great Lakes fishing industry, boat building, early agriculture—"

"Maybe more about people."

"Government? Church? Now, here's a good one about

127

the United Empire Loyalists, how they came to this part of the country."

Felicia remembered Ashley's claim and shook her head. "I mean like ordinary people, like me. Didn't people like me come to this country a long time ago, too?"

"Ah, yes." Mr. Allenby crouched down and ran his hand along the row of books. "Let me see." Then triumphantly he withdrew a book and handed it to her. "Here you go. And here are two more...and I think there was another one I wanted to show you here, too..."

"I think three's enough."

Mr. Allenby got to his feet. "I think you'll find those very interesting. They'll tell you all about the Underground Railroad. Actually, a lot of escaped slaves settled in Ontario. I think there was a settlement somewhere near here. If you don't have a computer at home, we can look for more information at our Internet station over there."

"Oh, okay. Thanks."

"Anytime."

When Felicia met up with the group at lunch they were talking about the play. "Guess what?" Felicia announced. "I talked to Mr. Butler and I'm going to be a singing pioneer after all!"

"*Thank you*," Dodie said emphatically. "It would have been sickening to perform with Cynthia."

"I would never have gone for the lead if I'd known I'd have to sing with Ashley," said Josh. "What am I going to do? This is going to be so humiliating in front of the whole school."

"You'll be okay," said Matt. "You worry too much."

"And every time I make suggestions to Mr. Butler, trying to improve the dialogue, he ignores me."

"That's because your ideas aren't good enough." Ashley stood before them, flanked by four of her disdainful supporters.

"Josh is a good play writer," said Felicia, the words popping out of her mouth unplanned.

"You would be the last person to know if a play is good or not," said Ashley. Cynthia looked down at Felicia, pretending to stick her finger in her throat and gag.

Ashley turned and walked away, her foursome like a military parade behind her.

"She's good at entrances and exits," said Matt.

"What is it with her?" Renate asked.

"Just ignore her," said Dodie.

"I can't ignore her," said Josh. "I'm stuck with her. We even have a scene where we hold hands and sing to each other!"

"Oh no!"

"Please!" The girls all started to laugh.

"It's not funny." Josh slumped in his chair.

When they returned to class, Miss Peabody introduced Sally, the first student to present her family history. Sally lowered a screen from the ceiling, then stationed herself beside a computer and, as one photograph followed another, described the arrival of her great-grandparents from Holland after the end of the Second World War. "They brought tulip bulbs with them and planted them here. This is a picture of their garden."

The screen glowed with a vibrant mass of color. In the midst of the blossoms, an oval pond collected water, which cascaded down into it over a wall of rock. There was a collective "ooh" from the class. Sally also had a pair of wooden shoes, called *klompen*. Everyone wanted to try them on.

Felicia started to worry about what her own story would be like. She couldn't think of something her classmates might want to see, like the shoes, and she wasn't sure if her family had differences that made them interesting.

After school Felicia came home to an empty house. Florence had started playing bridge with the neighbors every other Thursday afternoon. The television sat silently in its corner, and nothing simmered on the stove. Felicia settled at the kitchen table and unrolled the poster she had begun working on the night before. The painted tree filled up the whole space. It had a substantial trunk with graceful limbs that extended into finer branches and feathery leaves. She'd started to add miniature duplicates of her great-aunt's still life painting and the military medal. The poster looked good, but now she needed to think about how to present her family history. Her first thought was of her father, a shadowy figure, gone from her life before she was old enough to know him. A memory emerged of him sitting in a chair supported by pillows, almost too fragile to be approached by his rambunctious toddler, Felicia. No one would want to hear about that.

What else? She stood and walked to the fridge, poured a glass of milk and mounded cookies on a plate, sat again, rapped her pen against the pad, and stared down at the books Mr. Allenby had given her.

She started to turn pages, glancing at pictures and reading what was written under them. This was a history that she didn't know much about. Words jumped off the page: sad, work, hard, Africa, slave, chain. She pictured her ancestors barefoot, needing a bath, sweaty and dusty, frightened, resentful, exhausted, toiling in fields while their owners sat in the shade fanning themselves and sipping cool cocktails. She thought of the many white faces in her class. Would they really want to hear about that?

Time to get started. Felicia knew her great-grandfather was a porter on trains. That meant he wore a uniform and helped people with their luggage. But her grandmother had told her that he had helped organize a union, so he must have been smart and brave. She started to write.

CHAPTER 27
Flower

DR. SIMON FOLLOWED Wilfred into the house. The smaller children swarmed around them. The doctor patted each head, then raised his hand in greeting to the rest. He approached Mr. Jenson and squeezed his patient's hand in a gesture of reassurance, then lifted away the cloth covering the wound. "Good, good. I see small signs of healing."

"Really?" Mr. Jenson's eyes brightened.

"Thank you, Doctor!" exclaimed his wife. "Please sit down and join us for tea. The kettle is already on the stove and starting to boil."

The others settled at the table as she sliced bread.

"Tea will cure my thirsty throat," said Dr. Simon. He glanced at Gabriel. "How fares my other patient?"

Gabriel, seated in Flower's lap, looked up at Dr. Simon and began to wail. Cleo lifted him into her arms. "He seems well. Thank you, doctor."

"Coughing or fever?"

"No longer. And he eats well."

"Good...good."

Eldon asked, "How is Samuel?"

"His wound is also improving."

"What good news!"

Dr. Simon frowned. "I have bad news, too, I'm afraid." Flower's bread suddenly felt mealy in her mouth. She swallowed with difficulty and looked across the table at her father as the doctor said, "You must leave here."

"Slave catchers?" asked Eldon.

"Yes. We've been told they're on the move. Samuel has left us. We pray for him, and for you." He set his mug on the table. "I need to pass on information for the coming journey." Eldon, Cleo, and the doctor stepped outside. Flower stood in the doorway holding her brother in her arms. She saw her father bend his head, his ear close to Dr. Simon's mouth. Cleo frowned and nodded, her lips sometimes moving, intent on memorization.

Hettie asked her mother, "Can't Flower stay here with us?"

Flower turned back into the house. "No! I must be with my own Ma and Pa!"

"I don't want her to go."

"Stop talking nonsense. You two go outside and keep an eye on the boys."

Flower and Hettie sat together on the porch. "I wish you could stay here."

"I can't."

"Will you remember me?"

"Yes."

"I want to give you something." Hettie plucked a tiny yellow flower growing along the path, and she handed it to Flower. "Keep this. Whenever you look at it, you can think of me, your friend Hettie."

"And when you see the flowers growing here again, you can think of me, your friend Flower."

The girls helped Flower's father and Wilfred carry as much hay as they could to the barn, and then Mrs. Jenson called everyone in for a hastily prepared meal. Eldon ate quickly, excused himself from the table, and went back to the barn. He returned with a crutch he had fashioned from a tree branch.

"Aren't you a wonder?" Mr. Jenson grasped the crutch and pulled himself up to a sitting position, then swung his legs out from under the blanket and sat on the edge of the bed, short of breath with his efforts. Flower was alarmed with the noises he made, until she realized he was laughing. "Isn't that somethin'?" He hung his head and closed his eyes. "A little dizzy, but it'll pass." He struggled to his feet, stood up, and placed the support under one arm.

"Needs more rubbing to make it smooth," said Eldon. "I'd hoped to finish sanding it before we left."

"I can do that." The lame man took a few hesitant steps then returned to the cot. "Thank you."

"What a wonderful sight." His wife dabbed at teary eyes with her apron. "I was so afraid I'd never see you walk again." She turned to Eldon. "Thank you for all your efforts. And now I have to pack a few things for you to take with you. We'll miss you and your family."

Mrs. Jenson put a few biscuits, dried fruit, and a crock of water into a sack for Eldon to carry. Gabriel was once again settled in his sling, and everyone came out onto the porch to say good-bye. Hettie started to cry. Flower stood dry-eyed between her parents. Her father held one hand and her mother the other. They stepped off the porch and began to walk up the lane to the road.

CHAPTER 28
Felicia

FELICIA FIDGETED in her seat. Miss Peabody talked on. Soon the teacher would introduce her, and Felicia would have to stand at the front of the class and present the story of her family. She continued to make notes, half listening, and rereheared her talk. After the homework had been assigned, Miss Peabody said, "Time for another project. Felicia?"

"I just have to get something from my locker."

"Very well."

Felicia stood up too quickly and dropped a book on the floor. She ignored the few giggles as she retrieved it.

Felicia taped her poster to the front board and turned to address the class. She swallowed hard and introduced herself. A door opened. Mrs. Mackie came in and sat at the back of the room. "Don't pay any attention to me. I've heard these presentations are interesting. I thought I'd come and hear one."

Felicia started again. "My grandmother's family came

up to Canada from Virginia in the 1800s. I don't know exactly when, but I know it was before the American Civil War, which started in 1861. I've been researching the Underground Railroad. It wasn't a real train. It was a way for people to escape from slavery—they would hide in one house and rest for a bit, then they would be told how to find the next hiding place. They had to memorize the directions and look for clues along the way—a nail in the trunk of a tree, or maybe a group of trees near a bend in a river. Every house they reached was like a train station on the way to Canada. It was very hard and dangerous to make the journey, and a lot of people didn't make it, but my ancestors did.

"I don't know very much about my relatives who came here first because it was so long ago, and we don't have any records. But I painted this poster with portraits of the relatives I do know about. My great-great-great-great-grandpa was a blacksmith, and his son was a furniture maker. He made really good things. My Aunt Vi still has one of the chairs he made. His oldest son was a soldier in the First World War. He belonged to a special unit called the No. 2 Construction Battalion. They did all kinds of things. They rebuilt roads and bridges after they'd been damaged. He got killed, and the government sent our family a medal. My grandma still has it, but she said it was too precious for me to bring to school, so I've painted what it looks like here on the poster. My great-grandpa also wore a uniform, but he wasn't a soldier. He worked for the railway, and he helped organize a union so they'd get better wages."

Her classmates began to ask questions. Jack wanted to know all about the war medal. Miss Peabody stood up from her desk and peered at the artwork.

"This is really beautiful. I think the whole class should come closer to see it."

Felicia's classmates stood in line, admiring the painted tree, the extended branches adorned with a collage of paint, newsprint, calligraphy, and fabric, and the tiny painted portraits.

"Why are there faces in these tiny leaves? It looks like they're falling away."

"My grandma's aunt and uncle lost their two little daughters to scarlet fever. That's supposed to be them."

Renate pointed to one branch. "This looks like a painting of a painting."

"My great-aunt was an artist. My grandma didn't want me to bring the real painting, so I made a miniature copy of it."

Mrs. Mackie said, "I think the whole school would enjoy seeing this. Do you mind, Felicia, if we put it in the glass case outside the office, just for a few days?"

"Um, sure, okay." Felicia returned to her desk. She could hardly wait to go home after school and tell her mother and grandmother every detail of her presentation.

CHAPTER 29
Flower

FLOWER DIDN'T look back. She knew she would just see unhappy faces. It seemed they were always saying sad good-byes and leaving safe places for the unknown. The image of Aunty Lizzie's kind, loving face creased with grief was etched in her memory. Flower wondered if she would ever see her again and hoped that Aunty would run away, too, and follow them to freedom.

Her parents chanted memorized directions to each other as they walked along.

"A half-day on this road…"

"Follow the brook until it widens…"

"Past the marsh with the burned-out trees…"

They walked in a ditch, through tangles of weeds, trying to stay hidden. As the sun dipped lower in the sky, they moved into a grove of trees beside the road.

"I don't know if I should sit down," said Cleo with a sigh. "I'm afraid I won't have the wherewithal to get up again." She gave Gabriel a sip of water from the crock, had one herself, and passed it to Flower.

"Can we eat now?" asked Flower.

"A little." Cleo broke a biscuit into four pieces.

"Is this all?"

Cleo frowned, but before she could speak, Eldon said "Hush."

"What is it?"

"Don't you hear that?"

"No!"

"No need for fear. It's a good sound, running water."

"The brook?"

"I'll go and see." Eldon disappeared farther into the trees. He returned with a smile. "That's it. We follow it north."

The water was low. Flower hopped from stone to stone while her parents picked their way, choosing flat rocks when they could. The brook emptied into a wetland, remnants of blackened trees jutting up from it at odd angles. The ground became soggy underfoot, slowing their pace, and thorns and branches sometimes caught them in the face.

Eldon stopped abruptly, his hand raised. Far ahead was a dark building, set back among tall trees. "Wait here. I'll go ahead to see if it's safe."

He returned within a few minutes. "This is the place. Follow close behind me. There's a small river up ahead."

The sound of water became louder as they approached the building. A door hung on rusty hinges. It creaked as Eldon swung it open. They stumbled through it into a large open space, found a corner beneath a broken window, and sat, their legs giving way beneath them. Cleo nursed Gabriel as they ate their meal. Then they leaned against each other in an exhausted heap and slept.

Flower awoke to the sound of squeaks and chirps. She lifted her head from her mother's lap and looked up. The ceiling was high and beamed, the wooden supports meeting at a peak in the center.

"Ma, look at those strange birds. See how they get inside their wings. Some of them are hanging upside down."

Cleo made a face. "Those aren't birds, they're bats."

"Do they bite?"

Eldon said, "No. They're useful creatures. They eat the bugs that bite us."

Cleo stretched and yawned, handing Gabriel to her daughter. "I'm so stiff. I feel as if I've aged a hundred years."

Eldon was up and investigating their new quarters. "Come outside. We'll sit in the sun and have our meal, warm our bones at the same time."

Flower said, "I miss sleeping in the barn."

"The straw was a comfort beneath us," agreed Eldon,

"and the animals gave heat. When we get free, I'll build us our own house, and you'll have your own bed."

"Can we get straw here, Pa?"

"I don't think so. We'll find pine boughs and maybe some moss."

"What is this place?" Flower stepped outside onto a platform. Water flowed beside and underneath it, creating a rushing waterfall that eddied into a circle below.

"Stay clear of the edge!"

Flower stepped back. "Yes, Pa." A glance at the swirling water made her dizzy.

"Mind your brother. Let your Ma have some more sleep. I'll come back soon."

What if something bad happened and he never returned? "Where are you going?"

"Do as you're asked, daughter."

Flower came back into the building to see her mother wrap her shawl tight around herself. She fell asleep on the floor. Flower didn't think her father would mind if she took the baby out where it was warm. She set Gabriel on the ground and rolled a pinecone back and forth in front of him. He lifted it to his mouth and started to chew, so Flower threw it back into the bush, causing him to cry with frustration.

"Shush now. I'll sing you a song about an angel named Gabriel. He had wings, and he could fly wherever he wanted." Gabriel fell asleep, heavy in her arms. She came back inside, laid him beside his mother, then stood and looked out the window.

A figure moved in the trees. Flower looked carefully. It wasn't her father.

CHAPTER 30
Felicia

FELICIA TOLD her family all about the success of her school project, the poster now featured in a glass case just outside the office.

"All that hard work paid off," said Florence.

"I think I'll pop into the school tomorrow and have a look at it," said Delia. "Maybe I'll bring my camera. You could stand in front of it, Felicia. I wonder if the glass might create some glare."

"Mom, please don't come to school with your camera."

"Why not?"

"Because it would be grossly embarrassing."

"Why are your mother's actions so often embarrassing?" Delia said, not really expecting an answer.

"I'm going to wait until she brings it home," said Florence.

The next day, Felicia's friends didn't wait for her at lunch, and they didn't look up when she joined them with her sandwich.

"Are you going to watch the lunchtime play rehearsal?"

"Maybe," said Dodie.

"Dunno," said Renate.

Sophie didn't reply, avoiding Felicia's glance by looking at the table.

"I've got some brownies. My grandma made them. They're really yummy. Want some?" Felicia unwrapped the squares.

Only Dodie took one, with a muttered "thanks."

Before Felicia had finished her lunch, the three others scrunched their wrappings for the garbage and stood up together. "Going to the play," said Renate. They walked away, leaving Felicia alone. The library offered a place to read, so Felicia stayed there, feeling bad and flipping through magazines until it was time to return to class.

Josh caught up with her in the hallway. "How come you didn't come and watch us?" he asked.

Felicia felt grateful for his awkward interest in her. At least someone missed her.

"I had some reading to do in the library."

"Can you come tomorrow?"

"Sure."

After school, the four girls walked to the stable, Felicia frequently two steps behind. "Do you want to come to my place after riding and see the kitten? He's growing really fast; he's all fluffy and so cute."

"Um, we're kinda busy."

"Are you guys mad at me?"

The three girls exchanged glances but said nothing.

Little was said as they groomed their horses. Felicia was glad to start the lesson. Astride Star, she focused on keeping her feet in their stirrups, looking straight ahead at the target points, moving easily with her mount, she and Morning Star a team. She listened to her instructor's constant voice including her in the lesson. But when it was over, the others talked briefly, and only to each other. They left without saying good-bye.

The barn was quiet, with only the sounds of horses' breath, the chewing of hay, the scraping of a hoof. Felicia brushed Star with long strokes. "I think you're the best horse in the world."

The horse stood solid and accepting. Felicia looked into one dark eye. "Are the other horses ever mean to you? I think I saw a mark where you'd been nipped." Felicia checked the rump but the mark was gone. She remembered the photos of Star when she'd been rescued, so thin and dejected. Francine said that the horses hadn't been fed or even given water. They had to drink from a brackish pond or from puddles on the ground. "Why are people so miserable? There's no good reason for it." Felicia stopped brushing and stroked the horse's face with her hand. "Are you my best friend, maybe my only friend?"

"What's that?" Francine came out of her office.

Felicia separated strands of mane hair. "Nothing."

"You're all alone tonight. Where are the others?"

"They left."

"Without you? They never do that."

Felicia started to brush Star again, although her coat was glossy. She wished Francine would go away. She didn't want to have to answer any questions.

"Is something wrong?"

Felicia's throat tightened, sealing her words inside. She shook her head, putting down the brush and picking up a broom.

"Here, I'll do that while you put Star in her stall." Francine took the broom and gave Star a friendly slap on her rear. "Would you like a lift home? I have to get some groceries. I could swing by your place."

Felicia shook her head, trying to hide her face.

"Have you girls had a falling out?"

Felicia led Star to her stall and removed the lead rope and halter. The horse received one last pat before the door slid shut.

"Bring me a shovel, and we'll finish this up. You can

help me with the graining and watering, then I'll drive you home."

Francine's truck smelled like the barn, a mix of hay and animal hair. She brushed the seat clean for Felicia with her hand. "It's not a limo, but it gets me from A to B." There was a muted roar as the key turned in the ignition. "Muffler's packing it in."

Felicia settled in the seat, comforted by the rough warmth of the vehicle and her instructor's friendly chatter.

"I don't know what's going on with you and your pals, but remember, these things happen to everybody at some time or another."

"Did it ever happen to you?"

"Me? Hah! The horse nut, more interested in riding than wearing the latest fashions and knowing what was 'in' at the moment. Of course it happened to me, happened all the time."

"What did you do?"

"I had a horse named Apollo. He was so beautiful. We rode perfectly together—it was like magic. I had another friend who liked to ride. I decided I didn't care what the gang at school thought of me."

"Oh."

"Do you know what?" Francine didn't wait for Felicia's assent. "I think you just have to believe in yourself. You're a smart girl." Francine found a country music station on the radio. When a commercial came on, she turned down the volume. "And another thing. You're a very good rider."

"I am?"

"A natural."

"I like riding. It's a wonderful, powerful feeling. And I love Star."

"She's a beauty." The truck pulled up to Felicia's house.

Felicia dropped her gear on a chair in the front hall. The cat rubbed against her legs, but when she picked him up, he arched out of her grasp, leapt to the floor, and made straight for her grandmother's lap. Once there, he stretched one paw up toward Florence's face and began to purr.

"Even the cat doesn't like me!"

Florence set aside her mending and the cat. "What's wrong?"

"Everyone hates me!"

Florence opened her arms to her granddaughter. "Now then, tell me what's happened."

Felicia wept as she described the behavior of the girls.

"Why do you think they're acting this way?" Florence asked.

"I don't know."

"Girls! They'll probably be over this by tomorrow."

"I want to talk to my friends in the city. I wish we had

a computer and the Internet so I could chat with them all the time. Is it all right if I use the phone to call my friends?"

"Certainly, darling. You do that. It will make you feel better."

Felicia punched in Rosalee's number. Luckily Lenore was at Rosalee's house.

"I miss you two. What's new, what's happening?"

"Very exciting stuff. We're working together on a history project."

"That's exactly what I've been doing! What's yours about?"

"We're doing the 'Chinese Industrial State.' Can you believe it? It is so boring we are turning into stone."

"Ours was family history and the history of Plainsville."

"Poor Felicia. When are you coming down to escape it? Come and stay with us."

"Actually, why don't you two come up here? Our school is putting on a play, and I'm in it."

"Are you singing and dancing?"

"Singing, anyway."

"Good enough for us. We'll check with our parents and let you know."

"Please, please, please—I'm dying to see you. My Aunt Vi is going to be driving in from the city. Maybe she could give you a ride."

As Felicia said good-bye, she heard the loud slam of

a car door. Delia burst into the house, threw her purse and jacket on a chair.

"Now what?" asked Florence.

"The worst thing possible. I think I'm going to be fired!"

CHAPTER 31
Flower

FLOWER CROUCHED down below the window to where her mother and baby brother lay sleeping.

"Hey there!"

Flower sucked in her breath and held it.

"I saw you, I know you're there."

The voice penetrated Cleo's sleep. Her eyes snapped awake. "What?"

"There's someone outside."

Cleo scrambled to her feet, grasped Gabriel to her chest with one arm and held Flower with her other hand.

"Where can we hide?" Flower whispered her urgent question. They looked around the large, bare space.

"Outside. We'll find your father." They started for the door and then stopped in their tracks. Before them, in the opening, framed by the sunlight, stood a young boy.

"Good day." He smiled into the gloom. Cleo and Flower remained still, didn't respond. He stepped inside and dropped a sack over his shoulder and onto the floor. "I brought you supplies."

Flower drew close to her mother. "Supplies?" she said.

The boy opened the sack. "Blankets, two of them, and some bread."

Eldon appeared in the doorway behind him. "You brought us these things? Did your Pa send you?"

"Yup."

"Your name?"

"Not supposed to tell. It's a secret."

"That's right. I forgot. Thank you, and please thank your Pa."

"Actually, my name's Ned, short for Edward. My Pa is..."

"That's all right. We'll keep it a secret. We don't want your Pa to have any trouble."

Cleo ran a hand over one of the blankets. Gabriel peeked out from his sling. Ned smiled at him and held out a finger for the baby, who immediately grasped it.

"Why do babies always do that? They like to hold your finger." Ned smiled at Gabriel. "Do you folks know about this place?"

"Not a thing."

Ned told them it was an abandoned mill, once a busy place, owned by his grandfather. They followed him down slippery stone steps to the lowest level. There, the river water flowed by. "You can leave from here, and no one can see you."

"Into the water?"

"Or in a boat."

"Is this place a secret?" asked Eldon.

"Not really a secret, except no one ever comes here but me and my Pa. Someday Pa is going to start it up again. Now we just do some fishing." He turned to Flower. "Do you like to fish? There's a special place I go."

"I don't know how."

"I'll show you."

Flower looked to her father for direction. Eldon said, "Show me this place. It can't be far from us. Flower doesn't know how to swim."

Ned led them to a quiet pool. The water eddied lazily around three large rocks. Eldon nodded, satisfied that they were within shouting distance.

When he was gone, Ned asked, "What's your name?"

"Flower."

"Flower? Like the ones that grow in the garden? I'll show you how I can catch a fish with a flower." He picked up a long stick, removed a knife from a leather sheath on his belt, and began to trim one end.

"You have a knife?"

"I'm a boy, aren't I?"

"Yes."

"Why don't you get me a pretty flower, Flower." Ned pulled some string from his pocket and tied it to one end of the stick while she found a faded blossom. "That'll do." He attached it to a hook at the end of the string and plopped it into the water. They watched as it bobbed on the surface.

"Where's the fish?"

"You have to wait for it. Give it time to notice the bait."

"Do fish like flowers?"

"They think it's a bug. They like to eat bugs."

"Do you know how to swim?"

"Of course."

"What if you were swimming and a fish happened by, would it bite you?"

Ned laughed out loud. "No! I guess a snake might bite you."

"A snake?" Flower drew her feet up under her skirt.

"Look!"

Flower saw nothing at first, then a dark shape beneath the surface, the snap of an open mouth. Ned jerked back on the line and pulled the fish up onto the rock. Its scales gleamed in the sunlight. They watched as it flopped helplessly, gills opening and closing.

"It can't breathe!" Flower hated seeing the struggle for air. "Throw it back in the water." But Ned picked up a stone and brought it down hard on the fish's head. It twitched and then was still.

"Here's your dinner." He presented it to her with pride.

Eldon built a small fire, and the family enjoyed the

fish. Flower licked her fingers and remembered eating the squirrels that Samuel had caught.

They sat by the fire until dusk; then Eldon poured water on the flames, and they went back into the building. The blankets made their bedding down warmer and more comfortable. Eldon and Gabriel fell asleep immediately, but Flower and her mother lay awake. Flower described Ned's fishing expertise.

"He's a helpful boy," said Cleo.

"He thinks I'm silly, even my name, I think."

"You're not silly."

"Ma, tell me again how you chose my name."

"When you were born, I thought you were the most beautiful baby ever. I tried to think of the right name for such a baby. I looked outside at the wonder of nature and all of the flowers, and I decided that you were just like a perfect flower."

"And Gabriel?"

"When he was born, I thought he was like a little angel from heaven, so we called him Gabriel, after the angel."

They lay silently, listening to the breeze in the trees. "Ma, Ned said if we heard an owl's cry four times in a row, we were supposed to go down those slippery steps. His Pa will take us away in his boat."

"I know."

"I hope it's a good boat and doesn't fall apart."

CHAPTER 32
Felicia

FELICIA, DELIA, and Florence sat at the kitchen table, each with a mug of steaming hot chocolate.

"Now then, what's happened?" asked Florence.

Delia blew across the mug, rippling the brown fluid. "I sold a truck."

"Is that so bad?"

"I'm supposed to be Mr. Abbot's secretary, not a salesperson."

"So tell us," said Felicia.

"I was busy as usual, filing forms, typing letters, organizing sales packages. There was this man out in the lot, looking. He kept coming in, wanting someone to help him. I told him that Mr. Abbot was in the city, and I couldn't find Sid, the salesman."

"Did you suggest he come back later?"

"Yes, but he was persistent. He had his eye on a red truck, said he needed one for his business. I happened to know about that vehicle. Mr. Abbot had said it was a great deal for the right person. It occurred to me that this was the right person."

"And?"

"I couldn't help it. I started to tell him what Mr. Abbot had said—how sturdy it was, no rust, pretty good gas mileage. Before I knew it, he wanted to buy it."

"That's great, Mom."

"I know about the contracts. I prepare them all the time. He signed in all the right places. His credit check was perfect. We did the plates. I gave him the keys. He drove it off the lot."

"What's so bad about all that?"

"Sid came back from lunch and saw me organizing the file. He was furious, said he was going to complain to Mr. Abbot. He said I didn't know my place."

"There's no need for that kind of talk," said Florence.

"He sounds like a creep," said Felicia.

"I just hope I can get another job here. I'll need a reference."

"Anyone would be lucky to have you." Florence was indignant.

"That's true, Mom," said Felicia. "Everything was going so well for us. Now everything stinks. Maybe we can move back to the city."

"There's nothing else wrong, is there?"

Felicia cast a glance at her grandmother, who shook

her head, but Delia noticed this exchange. "Tell me. Don't keep things from me. I don't like it."

"Just a little girl trouble," said Florence.

"What kind of girl trouble? Are you talking about those girls you've been chumming with?"

"Yes."

"And?"

Felicia hung her head, her throat tightening, "They don't like me anymore."

"What makes you think that?"

"They won't look at me; they give each other looks, especially when I say something. They don't wait for me." Felicia's explanation ended in tears.

"There, there, aren't they foolish," said Florence.

Delia stood up and went to her daughter, hugged her tight. "They certainly are foolish. They're not worthy of your friendship."

Felicia accepted a tissue from her grandmother and blew her nose. "I don't know why they're acting this way."

"Maybe I should speak to their parents," said Delia.

"No, Mom! Please don't."

"They shouldn't be allowed to treat you like that."

"You mean to help me, but you'd just make it worse."

"I might make it better."

Felicia sat up and straightened her back, stuck out her chin. "I can handle it."

"Let her try," suggested Florence.

"I don't know. For a day or two only. Then I'm getting involved."

Felicia tried to hold on to her confidence. The next morning she dressed carefully for school, putting on the clothes that she liked and was comfortable in: jeans, her favorite long-sleeved tee, and a fleecy vest. Delia offered to drive her, and Felicia agreed. She would be spared the lonely bus ride. They pulled up in front of the school at 8:15.

"Kind of early, darling—do you mind?"

"No, it's okay. I can read or use the Internet in the library."

"I want get to work and speak to Mr. Abbot before Sid gets there."

"Good luck with all that."

"You too. Don't forget, you deserve respect from everyone."

"So do you, Mom."

"I'll tell you all about it when I get home."

"Okay."

"And I'll want to hear how your day went."

"Okay, Mom. See you tonight."

Felicia went straight to the library, but instead of finding Mr. Allenby there, Ashley and Cynthia stood behind the main desk. Ashley looked up as Felicia came through the door, placed something in a drawer, and closed it. "Here's the artist." Cynthia giggled.

"I'm just getting something to read."

"Too much studying isn't good for you. Planning any more posters?"

Felicia started to browse bookshelves. "No."

"Your friends were really impressed with your work, especially Sophie."

"What?" But Felicia was talking to an empty room. The library door clicked shut.

She stood and stared at the closed door for a moment, wondering what those two were talking about. Was her poster the reason her friends weren't talking to her? The door opened again, and Mr. Allenby greeted her with a cheerful smile. "You're just the person I want to see."

"I am?"

"Yes. Remember when we talked the other day and I told you I thought that escaped slaves had settled somewhere near here?"

"Uh huh."

"Well, I was right. And there's a Black History Museum that documents the settlement near Collingwood. I told Miss Peabody about it, and she's keen to plan a field trip to visit it."

"Cool."

"And I've got another book for you. It's about quilts and how people used them to signal which houses along the Underground Railroad were safe."

Felicia thanked the librarian and took the book with her. She started down the hall to class. As she passed the office, she and the principal almost collided. "Oops, sorry Mrs. Mackie."

"That's all right. We were both in a rush. Were you coming by to admire your project?"

Felicia smiled as they both turned their attention to the glass case beside the office door. Felicia stared in shock at her poster, slid the glass back, and reached in to remove it, wanting to lift it away before the principal could see it. She wasn't quick enough.

"What on earth?" Mrs. Mackie touched Felicia's hand, stopping it in midair. They both stood and looked at her work. At the top of the family tree, where Felicia had sketched a small portrait representing herself, was a photo clipped from a magazine. It showed a chimpanzee wearing a pink dress, grinning widely, showing every one of its teeth.

CHAPTER 33
Flower

THE SOUND of the owl came quite clearly the following night, four hoots and then silence. Eldon and Cleo were lying awake, but Flower struggled out of sleep, stood as the sack was tied on her back. The family gathered at the bottom of the slippery steps and looked down at the dark water.

Her father called quietly, "Hello. Anyone there?"

No one answered, but a flat-bottomed boat appeared below, and a hand reached up to assist Cleo with Gabriel, and then Flower, down into the boat. Eldon came next, and the craft moved forward. The night was dark and damp. Clouds scudded across the night sky, flying by the waning moon. Flower shivered and leaned up against her mother for warmth. The man managing the boat didn't speak. He sat on the middle plank, an oar in each hand. The boat lurched with each sculling motion. As they headed up the river, it became a greater struggle.

Eldon said, "I can sit beside you and take the other oar.

Two of us are better than one."

"I guess. The wind is getting up, making it hard." He moved to one side, and Eldon slipped onto the seat beside him, picking up an oar. They managed in this way for hours. Each time they stopped to catch their breath, the boat moved back, briefly canceling their efforts.

Just as the darkness began to ebb, the boatman said, "This is the place, and not too soon either." The craft moved out of the current and into a quiet cove. "Quick now, before you're seen."

Eldon put down his oar, shook his companion's hand. He stepped out into the shallows, assisted Cleo and the baby, and then carried Flower to the shore. "He'll have an easier time going home," said Eldon.

"Where are we?" asked Cleo.

They walked further into the bush, found a mossy spot surrounded by greenery, and sat down. Cleo pulled out the last biscuit and the remains of the fish. "We'll have a little of this and save some for later," she said.

"Maybe I can catch another," said Flower. "Ned showed me how."

"That would be good." Cleo gazed at the new morning. "Such a sky." The dawn light was a blaze of red, the glow reflecting on their faces.

"Take warning," said Eldon.

"What?"

"A proverb I heard once. 'Red sky at night, sailors' delight; red sky at morning, sailors take warning.'"

"That sounds scary, Pa."

Eldon didn't acknowledge her fear. "I'll scout out where we are and where we need to head next."

"Let's stay together," said Cleo.

"I'll return before you know it. You and Flower should look for some more fruit."

They had difficulty finding fruit-bearing bushes. It was late in the season, and the birds and animals had taken their share. Cleo and Flower picked what they could and waited for Eldon to return. The red sky was transformed, now gun-metal gray; the wind set the bushes waving, sent leaves twisting through the air, then scuffing along the ground at their feet. They huddled together, Gabriel between them.

"Where's that pa of yours? It'll be raining next."

By the time he arrived back, they were all soaking wet. Eldon led them to the shelter he had created. They lay beneath the slanted branches on cedar boughs and slept fitfully. Travel that night was made impossible by the relentless downpour. Thunder pounded around them, and shafts of lightning blasted the night darkness away.

It rained all the next day, becoming lighter late in the afternoon. "It's time we set out again," said Eldon.

"Oh, my bones are weary." Cleo stood and arched her back before bending over and picking up her baby.

They continued their journey. Flower walked behind her father, trying to match her steps with his. It was difficult—the rain had created mud that sucked at their feet and stuck to their shoes, making them heavy and harder to lift. The stones and tree roots were slippery obstacles, causing them to slide and trip.

"Eldon, I must rest." Cleo's voice was strained with fatigue. They sank to the ground beneath a tree. Each took a turn drinking water from their crock, and Cleo fed Gabriel. "Let's build us another shelter."

"All right, we'll stay for a bit, then try again."

"Are we lost?"

"No. We can still see the river. But it's better at night when we can follow the North Star."

"Too many clouds anyhow."

They got to their feet and started once more. Flower walked along, trying not to fall down. Her mind wandered to thoughts of Samuel. She imagined him struggling in the same direction. He would be afraid and alone. Maybe they would meet again and help each other. And Hettie—what would she be doing right at this moment? It felt like mealtime. Probably they were all sitting around the table, passing a basket of biscuits, spooning up warm soup. Flower almost cried out with hunger. She wanted something to eat, wished that her family was somewhere dry and safe, remembered the comfort of hay beneath her in a barn warmed by the bodies of farm animals. When her father stopped abruptly, she almost bumped into him.

"Is this the place?"

Eldon raised his hand for silence. They stood and looked at a cultivated field that bordered the forest. Several cows and two horses were grazing.

"The barn is red. Should it be red?"

"I don't recall being told that."

"Can we sleep in that barn, Pa?"

"Maybe. I have to find out. Stay quiet here and I'll scout."

"Don't leave us."

"I'll be right back."

CHAPTER 34
Felicia

FELICIA REMOVED the tacks from each corner of her poster, lifted it out of the case, and rolled it closed. As she turned to go, Mrs. Mackie stopped her.

"Wait. We have to deal with this."

"I want to put it in my locker."

"Not just yet. Let's go to my office."

Felicia had never been in the principal's office before. It had a large desk covered with papers and a bookcase topped with framed family pictures. A window looked out through evergreen shrubs to the street. Mrs. Mackie talked to the secretary, then came in and sat down.

"When was the last time you saw your poster?"

"Yesterday, after school, before I went to the stable."

"And did it have that picture on it?"

"No."

"So, this probably just happened this morning."

"I guess."

"Which is good. It means maybe no one saw it. It's too early."

"Yeah." It made Felicia feel better to know that a crowd of students hadn't gathered to laugh and jeer at her work.

"Has anything else bad happened to you lately?"

Felicia moved the zipper up and down on her vest. "No. I'm fine."

"I know this is very difficult for you, Felicia, but we can't let an issue like this slip by without dealing with it."

Felicia stared out the window. *This is the end of living here. Mom's going to lose her job, and I won't be able to ride Star anymore.*

Mrs. Mackie stood up and pushed back her chair. "Let's go to your classroom. Bring your poster."

"I don't want anyone to see it now."

"You're right. Open it up. We'll take off that horrid picture." The operation was done quickly, like a bandage peeled away from a scrape. "There. It's as good as new." Mrs. Mackie scrunched the offending picture and tossed it into the garbage. "Let's go."

Back in the classroom, Miss Peabody's usual smile faded when she saw their facial expressions. "Is something the matter?"

Mrs. Mackie spoke quietly to the teacher. "Felicia's poster has been tampered with. We've removed it from the glass case and she's put it away in her locker."

"Your lovely poster. How terrible. What shall we do?"

Felicia knew everyone in the class was riveted, trying to hear what the principal and the teacher were saying. "I want to go to my desk."

"Yes, of course, that's fine."

The principal and the teacher continued their whispered conversation as Felicia slipped into her seat. She pulled out a workbook and studied its blurred pages. A folded paper was taped to the inside of the back cover. Felicia opened the note and read:

> Roses are red
> Vilets are blue
> No one rides a horse
> As klutzy as you

There was a crude drawing of a scarecrow-like figure on a horse. It was signed 'dodie.' Felicia walked to the recycling bin and tore the note into little pieces.

The morning was a fog of grammar and geography. Just before lunch, Marie presented her family saga. She ended her presentation by passing around a tray of tiny cakes called *petits gâteaux*, and she described how she had made them the evening before, using her grandmother's recipe.

After class Felicia decided to speak to Dodie, who was

getting her lunch out of her locker. "Your note was really pathetic. I was going to correct the spelling and send it back to you, but I decided to rip it up."

"What are you talking about?"

"Don't act so innocent after all the mean things you've done." Renate and Sophie walked up to Dodie, robbing Felicia of some of her confidence. But she persisted, "Especially ruining my poster."

"I didn't touch your poster or send you a note."

"Well I got a nasty note this morning, and it was signed 'Dodie.'"

"I got a note too," said Sophie, "last week…from you, Felicia."

"I never sent you a note, Sophie."

"It was mean, too," said Sophie.

"It wasn't from me, really it wasn't," Felicia insisted.

"There was an ugly picture on it of me, too."

"Do you still have it?"

"No, but Ashley said you must have done it 'cause you're so good at art."

"Ashley told me you didn't like my poster."

"What?"

"She said something about you and my poster."

"I didn't say anything about the poster." The girls turned their attention to Ashley who was brushing her hair. "Did I, Ashley?"

Ashley gazed at her reflection in the mirror attached to her locker door. "Honestly! Can't anyone take a joke?"

"Jokes are supposed to be funny," said Felicia.

"I thought it was funny. We all had a good laugh watching you and your fellow geeky losers get so upset, didn't we?" Ashley turned to the group of supporters surrounding her. They all shared the same satisfied smirk.

Felicia said, "I think you're a little confused. You're the loser."

"Yeah!" added Renate.

"Yeah, you loser!" Sophie's face was flaming red.

Ashley shrugged her shoulders, glanced once more at her mirror, and closed the locker door. Felicia turned and walked away.

CHAPTER 35
Flower

FLOWER WAITED in the trees with her mother and Gabriel. Rain came down from every angle, sliding off leaves and dripping from branches. They shivered with cold and fatigue. Her father was taking a long time.

Suddenly a dog barked, its sound straining and whining with excited urgency. Flower looked up at Cleo's stricken face. "Ma?"

Cleo looked about her, frantic. "Run!"

They started to flee deeper into the forest. As before, their shoes stuck in the mud. It was an effort to lift each foot. Cleo stumbled and fell to the ground. Gabriel started to scream.

Flower helped her mother to her feet, gripping her hand as they stumbled over stones and tree roots, slipping and sliding, making hardly any progress. "Hurry. Hurry." Flower's command was whispered, like a prayer. Now they could hear the voices of men, their words indistinct but threatening. The sound of barking dogs was getting louder—agitated, impatient.

Cleo fell again. She looked up at her daughter and said, "Go on. Run away, while you can."

Flower stood suspended in time, saw men approaching them.

"Run! Run!"

She turned and scrambled between trees, up a hill. She could hear heavy footsteps behind her, a voice panting and cursing. A hand grabbed at her climbing foot. Flower kicked back and made contact.

"Ow! You little devil." She could hear him fall backward down the slope. Flower continued on until she reached the top of the hill. She hid in a bush, shaking and short of breath. She clasped her knees and buried her face in her skirt.

The voice moved away. "There's still one more. Where's the dogs when we need 'em?"

Flower shivered. The dogs would easily find her. Where could she be safe? Not in a bush. She crept out of her hiding place and looked down. Peering from behind a large rock, she saw her mother surrounded by three men. They were grabbing at her and shouting. Flower's decision was immediate and instinctive. She stumbled and scraped her way back, slid down the muddy slope, threaded her way through stands of trees and drizzling rain, back to Cleo.

She threw herself against her mother, encircled that thin body with desperation and love.

The men were jubilant. "We've got her! We've got the last one."

Flower was pulled away, her hands roughly tied behind her back, another rope around her middle, connecting her to Cleo. They were pushed and prodded, like herded cattle, back along the muddy track. The people at the farmhouse cheered as Cleo and Flower were brought back. The words weren't clear, just the roar of triumph.

Flower walked behind Cleo and focused on her bound hands and on Gabriel, curled within his sling, his face pressed against his mother's back. When they reached the drive, she saw her father, trussed with rope, lying on the ground.

Someone kicked him. Flower squeezed her eyes shut, but she could still hear the sound of boots thudding against Eldon's body, his groans, her mother's screams for them to stop. One of the men raised a threatening hand to Cleo but didn't strike her. He gave Eldon another kick.

"Yeah, that'll teach him."

"Know your place, boy."

"What'll we do with this lot?"

A woman's voice, "That one with the babe looks strong enough, the girl too. I could do with some help here."

"No. Take them to town. Let the sheriff look after it."

"Slaves are worth a lot of money. We could collect something if we return them to their master."

"Tracking down the owner sounds like a lot of trouble. Let's have our own sale."

"Good idea."

"They still need to be taken to town. Let's get this one on his feet." Eldon was pulled up from the ground, another rope lashed around his middle.

"Where's the wagon?"

"Coming." A wooden wagon harnessed with one horse pulled up in front of the house. Eldon, Cleo with Gabriel slung to her back, and Flower were tied in a row behind it. The driver flicked the whip, and the horse started forward. Flower fell to the ground with the sudden motion. She could hear laughter as she struggled awkwardly to her feet.

One voice was sympathetic. "She's just a little girl."

"Hah! That one gave me a kick. She needs to learn a lesson."

The wagon moved forward again, and the family stumbled behind it. Flower was pushed to keep up. On the road, the horse started to trot, and Flower fell again, scraping her face. The horse's gait was kept to a walk, but after a while, Cleo fell with Gabriel, and then Flower again. The driver stopped and stepped down from the wagon. He allowed Cleo and the children to ride, but Eldon was made to follow behind for another hour. Flower couldn't look at her struggling father. She tried to block out what was happening to him with prayer, but the words were jumbled in her mind.

They finally arrived at the outskirts of a town, and the wagon stopped in front of a stone building. The driver went inside and returned with another man, who looked at the desperate group and asked, "What have we got here?"

"Runaway slaves, a whole family."

CHAPTER 36
Felicia

FELICIA WALKED along the hall after French class, silently memorizing verb endings. Lucy and Cynthia came up behind her, then beside her, forcing her in their direction.

"Excuse me!" Felicia tried to slip away, but they pressed closer against her and quickened their pace.

The girls' washroom was the last door on the left at the end of the hall. Felicia was steered into the tiled space with the two girls flanking her. The only sound was the dripping of a tap. Then Ashley and Melissa jumped out from behind the open door. "Boo!"

Felicia drew her breath in sharply, but managed not to cry out. She was surprised to see Melissa. She had always found her to be quietly pleasant.

"Party time," said Cynthia. Felicia could smell bubble gum on her breath.

"You mean makeover time."

"And here's our little guinea pig."

Felicia didn't move, eased out a breath. Her pulse

pounded in her head. She started an inward count to ten. They mustn't see her fear. *One...two...*

"She needs a new look."

"Her hair's so ugly."

They sauntered in a circle around her. *Three...four...*

Cynthia and Ashley shared a mean smile. "We have ways," Ashley lifted a pair of scissors from her pocket and clicked the blades together, "to make changes."

"For the better."

Ashley advanced and waved the scissors back and forth above Felicia's head. "Now let me see."

"Don't! Don't touch me!"

"Maybe this one." Ashley tugged at a braid.

"A good one," agreed Cynthia, "right at the front."

"Stop it!" Felicia backed into Lucy, who pushed her forward.

The squeak of rubber-soled sneakers on tile stopped the action. Ashley raised one eyebrow and angled her head toward the doorway. The girls filed out, leaving Felicia breathless in the washroom. She turned to the sink and washed her shaking hands as Sally entered a stall.

Instinctively, Felicia sought out the most public place in the school, the auditorium, where the play was being rehearsed. She sank into a seat amid a group of other students. Mr. Butler stood on the stage, surrounded by cast members.

"We're on page twelve. Matthew is playing the Reverend. It's the Thanksgiving scene. Everyone? It's page twelve."

Felicia practiced her deep breathing and focused on Matthew's reading. After the run-through, they left the auditorium together. She said to him, "Hey Matt, you were good."

"You're blinded by my acting skill."

"I guess so."

Felicia said good-bye and set out for the stable. She heard footsteps behind her, then Dodie's voice. "Felicia, wait up."

Felicia turned to face them. Dodie was grim-faced, determined. She and Renate exchanged glances; and then Dodie said, "We decided we should talk."

"Okay."

Sophie stepped forward, her freckles vivid against her pale face. "I thought you'd done something mean to me, and I was wrong."

Felicia almost replied that's okay, but stopped and considered what she really wanted to say. "You were all so mean to me."

"I know," said Sophie, "and it's my fault."

"No it's not. It's all our faults," said Renate.

"Why didn't you talk to me?" asked Felicia. "If only you'd asked me, I could have told you…"

"I was too embarrassed. The picture was so horrible."

"So was mine." Felicia was reminded of her own reaction to the defacement of her work—how she wanted to hide it from everyone, as if it were a terrible secret that no one should know about. "So, are you still mad at me?"

"No. We feel bad," answered Renate.

They started to walk together. Felicia found she had many unsaid things roaring around in her head. A spasm of lingering anger made her twitch. "It was so hard when you wouldn't speak to me."

"I know," said Renate.

"No, you don't."

"Yeah, I do. One time last year, Sophie and Dodie got mad at me. I was so upset. I didn't know what to do."

"I'm sorry, again. I feel so guilty," said Sophie. She started to cry.

"Come on, Soph, don't be such a suck," said Dodie.

Renate put an arm around Sophie's shoulder. "You're too sensitive."

"It was different for me," said Felicia. "You treated me different, because I am different."

"No we didn't."

"It sure felt like it. It felt like the way Ashley and her group treat me. Like I don't belong."

"We're not racist, you know!"

"Yeah. We're not like that."

"Honest?"

"Honest."

"This is what I think," said Dodie. She stopped walking as she spoke, and the other three stopped with her. "I think we all know what it's like when your friends are mad at you and won't speak to you, right?"

"So?"

"So, I think we should promise each other that if something like this happens again, we get together and say what's wrong."

"Then the person might be more upset. It could get worse."

"Maybe," said Felicia. "But it would be better than nobody talking."

"Okay?"

"Okay."

"Let's go."

Francine greeted them as they trotted up the drive to the barn. "Looks like there's lots of energy here—good."

"Why good?" asked Renate, breathless.

"Because I want to try some real synchronized riding today, and I was hoping you'd be up for it."

"All right!"

The exercises were complicated. The girls practiced one at a time, then with two riders, and finally with all four of them, circling in each corner of the arena, crossing at the center and then back to the corners, and then riding in twos up each long side. Their past antagonism was forgotten in the shared rhythm of the exercise. After the lesson, Fran smiled up at Felicia. "Did that feel good?"

"Yes. Star is so great. She knows just when to turn."

"Give yourself some credit. She knows when to turn because you are telling her with your riding."

Felicia stroked the long neck, leaned forward, and whispered into one whiskered ear, "You are the best."

The students hopped off onto the sawdust, loosened the girth straps, and ran up the stirrups. Their horses were toweled and each given a carrot, except for Cecil, who preferred peppermints.

Felicia and Sophie went into the tack room together to return the saddles and hang up the bridles. As she unbuckled straps, Sophie said, "Felicia…"

"Yeah?"

"I'm so glad it wasn't you who made that awful picture of me."

"What was the picture?"

"It was supposed to be me, but it was that ugly clown puppet with red hair and freckles. The one that murders everybody."

"No!"

"What was yours?"

Now it was Felicia's turn to relive the humiliation. "It was a monkey wearing a pink dress."

"That Ashley is so…"

"Is so what?" Ashley and Cynthia swept into the tack room. Ashley lifted a saddle off its post and stood glaring at Felicia and Sophie. Cynthia looked at the floor.

Felicia found her voice. "Is so immature."

CHAPTER 37
Flower

THE MARSHAL looked at the disheveled family in the wagon. "What am I supposed to do with this bunch?"

"Lock them up. They've broken the law, run away."

"So send them back to their owner."

"And who would that be? We're thinking we'll have our own sale. They can stay here till we're ready."

"How long will that take?"

"Don't know. Not long, I expect."

The marshal sucked on his teeth and sighed through them.

"Get down, then, all of you." Cleo stood shakily, swayed a bit on her feet. Flower stood up and put her body against her mother's, trying to support her. Gabriel stayed scrunched and silent in his sling. The marshal and the driver reached up and helped them down, but offered no assistance to Eldon, who stumbled clumsily, his wrists in a bloodied knot behind his back. A small crowd gathered to watch as they were shepherded into the jail. One man spit at them, his saliva splatting at Cleo's feet.

"That's enough now," said the marshal to the assembled group. "Go on back about your business."

The family was directed into a small cell. The door slammed behind them as they shuffled in. Cleo and Flower collapsed on a cot chained to one wall, Eldon on the opposite one. Flower could see a small window high up in the center, revealing a square of cloudy sky.

Cleo asked, "Please, Sir, could you free me? My babe needs tending to."

The marshal was hanging keys on a hook. He turned and looked at them with surprise. "There's a babe, too?"

"Yes, Sir, in the sling on my back."

"Just a minute while I go and fetch my deputy." He left them alone as he set out to get assistance. Flower and her mother sat quietly, trembling with exhaustion and despair. Through the window they could hear the din of everyday activity on the street. Men's voices, rough and argumentative, became louder. The door opened and four men entered the jail.

"There they are."

"I told you, didn't I?"

"They look healthy enough."

"Worth a good amount."

"Especially him."

"I told you."

"The woman has a babe."

"They should be kept together, for a while anyway."

"I like the look of that young girl."

"Kinda scrawny."

"Bring her out. Let's have a look."

Flower's heart beat like a wild bird in her chest. She watched as one of the men searched the sheriff's desk drawer until he noticed the keys hanging on a hook on the wall. "Here's what we want." He fumbled until he found the key that unlocked their cell door, opened it, and entered the small space. He yanked Flower to her feet and drew a large hunting knife from his belt. With malignant precision, he cut the rope binding her to her mother. She was led out of the cell and presented to the others.

"Hard to tell what's what when she's covered with mud."

"She moves good."

"How old do you think she is?"

A brutish hand touched her chest, pinched it hard. Flower gasped with the sudden pain but didn't cry out. "Still a girl."

"Girls grow fast."

"Please, Sir," Cleo pleaded, her voice ignored.

"Can we take what we want now before the sale?"

"Wouldn't get away with it."

Their discussion was interrupted by the return of the marshal with his deputy. "What's going on here? What do you think you're doing?"

"Just having a look."

"You can quit looking right now and be on your way." Flower was pushed back with her family.

"We weren't doing anything wrong."

"Breaking the law was what you were doing. Entering a public place, unlocking prisoners, interfering with the due process of…"

The men turned to go, surly and unrepentant. "Yeah, we're the public."

"Get on out of here, or I'll be finding a cell for the lot of you."

Flower sat silent and numb after her ordeal. She watched as Cleo was released and Gabriel lifted from his sling. Cleo embraced him and rocked him back and forth, humming a frantic, tuneless song, then extended one arm to include her daughter in a mournful hug.

Later, the deputy brought them water, then bowls of broth and some bread. Flower and Cleo tried to eat, but their ravenous hunger of hours before had left them, and they weren't able to swallow. Eldon remained on his cot, his face to the wall. He didn't acknowledge the offering of food.

The night sky darkened, and the noise increased as many people gathered outside the building. The marshal and his deputy paced back and forth, stopping every once in a while to check the view from the window. They talked together, lifted keys from the hook, and placed them in the bottom drawer of a desk. Both men checked that their firearms were loaded and ready.

Flower listened to the roar of people outside and knew that she was as helpless as an animal caught in a trap. Tomorrow they would be sold. Their family would be torn apart. She remembered the tragic story Aunty Lizzie had once told her—of how she had been sold as a child to Master Chesley, how she had stood on a platform as voices had called out in a rapid blur, and how her mother had howled in despair.

Light flickered on the ceiling from the torches outside. Men yelled to each other and sang snatches of song. There was harsh laughter and the occasional sound of crockery breaking. Inside, the marshal and his deputy leaned back and dozed in their chairs. Cleo rocked and hummed and prayed. Flower looked across the cell at her father, their pillar of strength. He lay silent and still, staring at the wall but not seeing it, like something broken.

CHAPTER 38
Felicia

FELICIA FOUND her grandmother sitting in front of the television, the kitten curled in her lap. "Does that cat ever lie anywhere else?"

"You're sounding a little grumpy, darling. Things still bad at school?"

"He needs to learn to have some independence."

Florence eyed her granddaughter, but addressed the little cat. "Is it time you learned to be independent? I don't know—you're still awfully tiny." She lifted him up in the air as she spoke to him, and he meowed in return.

Felicia headed for the kitchen. "I'm starving."

"I baked some cookies, but have an apple first."

Felicia was about to protest having fruit but couldn't be bothered. She lifted one from the bowl in the middle of the table and bit into it. It was agreeably crunchy, and a spurt of juice filled her mouth. She walked back into the living room and flopped down on the couch. "Don't you ever get sick of watching these game shows?"

"No. I find it fun, and I try to come up with answers. Keeps my brain working."

Felicia listened to the program. "Ugh, history, who cares about that?"

"Hush now, I think I know this. What was his name? Alexander, Alexander, um, Alexander Graham BELL!" There was a buzzer blast as Florence's correct answer coincided with the contestant's response on the program.

"Who's he?"

"He invented the telephone that you love so much, and he worked on it here in Canada."

"Yeah?"

"See, not so boring."

Felicia turned her attention to the cat, now sitting up and licking one paw. He sensed her attention, stopped what he was doing, and stared across the room. "Nana, can I hold the kitten for a while?"

"Sure. Come and get him."

"He probably just wants to stay with you."

"Try him."

Felicia reached across and lifted the fluffy bundle into her arms. He looked back at Florence and then nestled in as his head was stroked. "Have you decided on a name?"

"I think so. How about Rufus?"

"That wasn't on the list I made for you, Nana."

"I know. It just came to me. Do you like it?"

"It's all right." Felicia slipped a braided bracelet off her wrist and offered it to the cat. He began to pummel it with his front paws. "I guess it's a cute name—sounds fluffy, like he is."

"Rufus it is then. What's that folded up in the corner?"

"My poster."

"Oh, Felicia, show it to me. I never saw the final version."

Felicia set the kitten on the floor, rolled the bracelet across the carpet, and watched as he scampered after it. "Here it is, Nana."

"Let's take it to the kitchen where I can see better." They settled in the other room and opened the poster up on the table. Florence traced her finger over each picture on the family tree, reviewing names, nodding in admiration. "You've got it. You've got the gift."

"I've got the what?"

Florence raised her head and looked at her grand-daughter. "You've got the gift, just like your great-aunty, the gift of making art."

"Really, do you think so?"

"Yes I do." Florence's finger found the slight abrasion of the paper where the photo had been taped. "What's happened here?"

"I don't know, um, nothing." Felicia propped the poster on the sideboard and sat at the kitchen table.

Florence poured a glass of milk and offered the cookie jar. "Sweets for the sweet."

"Nana," Felicia swallowed a mouthful of milk, "did you ever, were you ever...?"

"Did I what?"

"Did you ever have anyone be mean to you, for no good reason?"

"Yes, I have, but not very often." Florence was thoughtful. "Are you thinking the reason might be because of your color?"

"I think so."

"Something happen?"

"This awful girl, Ashley, and her friends—they were going to cut off some of my hair. She had scissors."

"No."

"And she passed mean notes to my friends and put my name on them. That was why they stopped talking to me."

"That's terrible."

"And she was the one who tried to wreck my poster."

"We'll speak to the school. No one should get away with behaving like that."

"I saw her parents coming out of the principal's office yesterday. They didn't look happy."

"So things are straightened out?"

"Yeah, but I still feel bad that my friends believed her. How could they? They didn't speak to me for days."

"But everything's all right now?"

The front door opened and closed. Delia entered the kitchen and sank into a chair. "What a day."

"I'll make some tea," said Florence. "Have a cookie."

"I have a bit of a headache."

"I'll get you an aspirin, Mom." Felicia started for the stairs.

"Put the kettle on while you're up," suggested Florence. She turned to her daughter. "Did you speak to your boss?"

"I tried, but he was in and out of the place, and that Sid kept giving me stuff to do. Every time I turned around there was some other silly thing on my desk." Delia rubbed her fingers against her forehead. "I've been staring at a computer screen most of the day."

Felicia returned to the kitchen with a pill for her mother, drew a glass of water, and set them both on the table. "Take this."

"Oh, she's a nurse now." Delia chuckled and swallowed her medicine.

"Nana says I'm an artist."

"That's even better."

They raised their heads to the sound of a car door slamming. "Who's that now?"

Delia stood up and walked to the window. "Oh no! It's Mr. Abbot, my boss."

CHAPTER 39
Flower

THE DOOR of the jailhouse creaked open. The marshal and his deputy sprang awake, stood poised for confrontation. Flower watched from behind the grill of the cell door as one man, dressed in black, came in.

"There's been a request. I'm to examine those up for sale."

The marshal shrugged his shoulders, opened the bottom drawer of the desk, and lifted out the keys. "Not sure 'bout this."

Flower sat frozen with fear. Was she to be led out now and taken away? She looked over at her father, but he lay still as before.

"This man's going to check you all out," said the marshal. Flower stared at her clenched fists. A black bag appeared on the floor at her feet. The doctor opened it and lifted out a bell-shaped instrument. Cleo stopped humming and rocking. Flower felt a gentle hand placed on her head, looked up into the concerned face of Dr. Simon.

"Stay calm," he whispered. He added in a louder voice, "It's the custom before a sale to make sure everyone's in good health."

"Whatever you say." The marshal slumped in his chair, tipped his hat over his eyes. "The sooner this is over, the better."

"I understand there's a babe to be seen," said Dr. Simon. Cleo unwrapped Gabriel with clumsy fingers. He lay in her lap like a puppet whose strings have been snipped. Dr. Simon placed the instrument against the little chest, frowned as he listened. "Is he feeding?"

"Not for a while." Tears slid from Cleo's eyes, tracking down her dusty cheeks. "We've been treated so harshly. I think he knows, even though he's just a baby."

The doctor's face darkened with anger. He said to the two dozing outside the cell, "Here now! This mother requires nourishment if she's to provide some for her infant."

"She got some soup. They all did. It was wasted. They ate none."

"Bring some more."

"This here's not a café." The deputy rose from his chair, walked to a cupboard, and brought the same bowls of broth. Flower and her mother held them with disinterest.

"Drink that down," said Dr. Simon, "for strength." He turned his attention to Eldon, spoke his name quietly, but

Eldon did not respond, even as his bruised body was examined. Cleo quickly finished her soup. She rocked Gabriel and tried to feed him, singing and urging him to try, but he lay quietly and looked up at his mother with dull eyes.

"Is there a spoon available?" asked Dr. Simon.

"What next!" The deputy pulled a spoon from the cupboard, poked it through the cell bars.

Dr. Simon passed the spoon to Flower. "Try to give the baby some of this broth." He watched as she brought the spooned liquid to the baby's mouth and crooned to him, ladling a small portion into his mouth. Most of it dribbled out onto his cheek, but he did swallow some. "A capable big sister you are. The babe will soon be himself again." He continued in a low, hushed voice, close to her ear. "Listen for the message, then lead your family out the far passage. Helping hands wait there." He stared hard at her, then reached for her hand and slipped something cold and solid into it. She looked down to see a key, and slipped it quickly into the pocket of her aporn. Dr. Simon stepped outside. The door clicked as it locked. He dropped the ring of keys into the desk drawer and then spoke to the marshal, not looking back at Flower. "They seem to be fine, in spite of everything."

The lawman sat forward, yawned, and raised the brim of his hat. "We had nothing to do with that. I put them in the cell for safekeeping soon as they arrived."

Dr. Simon asked, "How is your own health?"

"My shoulder gives me pain the odd time." He raised his arm and rotated it in the air. "I can tell the change in the weather just by what my shoulder's saying. Could it be the arthritis?"

"Something which gives many of us cause for complaint. I have here what you might call an elixir, known to cure many an ailment. It might ease your soreness."

The deputy raised his head. "With me, it's the knees. They hurt like a son of a gun on a rainy day."

Dr. Simon lifted a bottle of brown liquid out of his bag. The deputy jumped up to the cupboard and returned with glasses, which were then filled halfway to the brim. The two men lifted their glasses to acknowledge the doctor and then swallowed in one gulp.

"That's the ticket!" The marshal coughed and tapped his chest with his fist.

The deputy laughed and asked, "Any more where that came from?"

"Mustn't overdo it," said Dr. Simon as he poured once more into each glass.

The men savored their remedy this time and sipped slowly. The marshal swished the fluid around in his mouth. "My shoulder's starting to feel better already."

"Say, Doc, any chance you can leave us some of this 'medicine'?"

Dr. Simon held the bottle up to the light and swirled the contents. "It's almost empty. Save the remains for a rainy day."

"We're mighty thankful."

"I must leave." Dr. Simon stood up.

The marshal's voice was friendly. "Drop in anytime when you're in this part of the county."

"Don't be a stranger," added the deputy.

Flower watched and listened. Dr. Simon slipped out the door, and the two men returned to their chairs. The deputy held the bottle up to the light once more, shook it, and then poured the rest of it into their glasses. They chuckled and talked as they sipped it. She continued to drip broth into Gabriel's mouth. He whimpered, and Cleo hugged him against her. "I have to keep trying to feed him, Ma." Cleo loosened her grasp and watched the broth, drip by drip, enter her baby's mouth. Flower didn't tell her mother she had the key. The doctor must have removed it from the ring. She wondered how he had managed that. And what had he meant about a message?

CHAPTER 40
Felicia

MR. ABBOT HESITATED before acting on Delia's friendly invitation to come inside. "Welcome, welcome."

"I'm awfully sorry to bother you at home. You're probably wanting to put your feet up after a busy day, but I thought we should have a talk."

"It's no bother. We were just going to have a cup of tea. Come into the kitchen and meet my family."

"Thank you. That's very nice of you." He smiled at Felicia and Florence as he entered the kitchen. Florence returned his smile, but Felicia attempted a haughty nod, similar to those so often administered by Ashley.

Felicia was asked to prepare the tea as the threesome at the table discussed the weather. She watched the kettle start to boil and felt anger simmering inside of her. *How dare this balding, potbellied man control our lives! He may be lucky enough to own a bunch of used cars, but he doesn't even have the brains to recognize Mom's intelligence, not to mention her amazing work ethic. How many sick days does she ever take? None, that's how many, no matter if she has the worst cold.*

"Felicia, dear, the kettle's boiling."

"Oh, yeah." Felicia donned an oven mitt to pour the bubbling water into the teapot, then clattered mugs and spoons on a tray. She paused in front of the cookie jar. Did this man deserve a cookie, handmade by her grandmother? Four cookies were grudgingly placed on a plate and set in the middle of the table.

"A few more please, and the bowl of fruit that's sitting on the counter, and plates and napkins," Florence said.

Felicia did as she was told. Delia poured tea, offered milk and sugar. "Or do you prefer lemon?"

"Just a little milk and one spoon of sugar." Mr. Abbot bit into a cookie. His eyes almost sparkled. "Delicious," he said, stirring his tea.

The conversation progressed from the weather to the expansion of the library and recent roadwork in town.

"It seems to take forever to get something done around here."

"Maybe we're in too much of a hurry."

"There's often a lack of skilled trades people."

Their talk washed over Felicia as she sat and studied her mother, marveling at her ability to disguise her anxiety. Delia sipped at her tea and offered delicacies to this rotund man who was about to disrupt their lives.

"Mom's always been admired for her organizational skills." Three heads turned to her in surprise. Felicia continued, "She won the history prize when she graduated from high school."

Mr. Abbot said, "That's something to be proud of."

Now Delia looked flustered. "It was a long time ago."

Felicia steamed ahead. "She doesn't get the credit she deserves. Why, once…"

Florence intervened. "Yes, we are proud of Delia's accomplishments, and that's not just family pride talking. Here, have another cookie."

"When she sprained her ankle, she still went to work, even though the doctor said she should sit with her foot up on a pillow."

"Dear me, Delia, when was that?" asked Mr. Abbot, a line creasing his forehead.

"So long ago, I can hardly remember." Delia tried to give a meaningful look to her daughter, who avoided eye contact.

"People are only supposed to work eight hours a day, aren't they?"

"Felicia, I think it's time for our favorite program." Florence looked up at the clock on the wall.

"What favorite program? I don't—"

"You know which one I mean." Florence got to her feet. "Come and give me a hand, that's a good child."

"I don't…oh, okay." Felicia followed her grandmother into the front room. "I wanted to keep talking."

"Let your mother do the talking. She's capable." Florence eased into her chair and clicked on the television.

"That man is too fat. He needs to go on a diet," said Felicia. Florence turned up the volume. "Eating up all our good cookies."

"We'll make some more."

"Mom shouldn't have to be alone with him."

"Hush, child, and pay attention to the program. It's educational."

In the kitchen, Delia and Mr. Abbot faced each other across the table. Mr. Abbot cleared his throat. He started to speak, having to raise his voice over the sound of a television narrator describing the patterns of killer-whale migration. And in the living room, Felicia strained to listen to the conversation in the kitchen.

She finally heard her mother walk Mr. Abbot to the front door. He poked his head into the living room as they passed. Felicia jumped up and hugged her mother.

"A fine family you have, Delia," said Mr. Abbot.

Delia disguised a poke to her daughter, who un-wrapped herself. Felicia knew the poke meant "stand up straight and remember your manners." Mr. Abbot made his way out the door and down the walk to his car.

"What happened?"

"Sometimes things work out all right."

"Do you still have a job?"

"Yes, and more responsibility, and maybe even some more money. Seems I can try my hand at selling cars. But I still have to do the clerical work."

"That sounds like a lot," said Florence.

"Will that Sid guy still be mad?"

"I hope not. But I can deal with that. He'll just have to get unmad."

CHAPTER 41
Flower

FLOWER FOCUSED on her baby brother until he no longer swallowed, and the broth dribbled out onto his cheeks. She wiped them with her sleeve. "He's asleep now." Cleo wrapped him in her shawl and began to hum again. Eldon lay silent on the other side of the cell. Flower briefly lowered her tired head onto her mother's lap, but Cleo's incessant rocking made her sit up again. She approached the barred entrance to the cell and looked out beyond it.

The jail was dark except for a hanging oil lamp, which cast a pool of light over the marshal's desk. His head lay upon the desk top, buried in his folded arms. The deputy sprawled back in his tilted chair, his legs splayed out in front of him. He was snoring, but the marshal made no sound. Flower had seen them drink the "medicine," and she hoped they were deeply asleep. She put her hand through the bars and around to the lock. It would be awkward, but she thought she could unlock the door from the opposite side.

The desk with the sleeping lawmen stood in the center of the room. On a sidewall was a cupboard, and beside that was another door, slightly ajar, darkness in the space behind it. Flower stood and studied the scene, then returned to the cot. She lay down beside her rocking mother and then gave in to her exhaustion and briefly fell asleep.

Dream voices entered her slumber: angry voices, voices that demanded and complained and threatened. She didn't want to leave her mother, clung desperately to her, but was dragged away, forced to climb stairs to a waiting platform. Hands poked and grabbed as she tried to resist.

Flower jerked awake, her body stiff with fear, jaws and hands clenched, her breath coming in little gasps. She moaned, reached over and touched her mother. They were still together. Flower lifted her head to see the lawmen deep in slumber. She could hear voices coming from outside, men talking.

"Now who would this be?" asked one of the men.

"Told you. No need to post the sale. Word of mouth's enough."

"People will come from all over."

"Out of the woodwork."

"Some just curious."

"Looking for entertainment."

"Don't want too many; it'll drive up the price for the rest of us."

"True. Unless you're selling."

"What's that man doing?"

There was the sound of footsteps climbing. "Someone's getting up on the platform! Who's that, the auctioneer?"

"We're not having one. Jeb's doing it."

"Hey, you up there! Planning to be part of the sale?" This question was followed by shared laughter.

"I bring a message." Flower sat up. There was something familiar about that voice.

"It's a little early for speech making. Wait awhile; you'll have a bigger crowd."

"The Lord speaks to everyone, through his messenger."

"A man of the cloth. Hey, preacher, it's not Sunday."

"Goodness does not wait for a special day."

"We're good most of the time." More laughter. "Well, some of the time."

"Now is the time to move on from your evil ways."

"We've heard enough. You move on. We've got business to conduct here in a few hours." This voice was louder, more authoritative.

"Business is what you call it. I call it the work of the devil."

"Call it what you like. Just don't bother us with your sermons."

Flower sat on the edge of the cot, listened intently. "Stop your humming, please, Ma." Cleo looked up with dazed eyes and stopped. "Listen," said Flower.

"The time has come to recognize the evil that is slavery. We are all brothers under our skins. It is wrong to sell your brother as if he were livestock."

"Mind your own business! We look after them, feed them, and house them for their work."

"A man should be paid for his work, not have to depend on others for the necessities of life. All men are equal unto the Lord."

"Ma! That man that's speaking…it sounds like Mr. Pemberton. Maybe he's going to help us." Cleo lowered her head and shook it side to side.

The shouting outside grew louder and angrier. "We don't want any interference! Get down from there and be on your way."

"I'm here to help you—to bring a message, to lead you on the path of righteousness."

"We can find our own way, thank you very much."

"Put your trust in the Lord and his messenger."

Flower noted the repetition of the word "message" and felt sure it was meant for their ears more than for the sullen crowd outside. "Listen, Ma. Listen to what he's saying. I think he's saying it to us." Cleo stopped rocking and leaned forward. Flower whispered to her father, "Pa, Mr. Pemberton is outside. He's talking to those bad people, but his words are meant for us to hear."

Eldon rolled onto his back, then, with effort, pushed himself upright into a sitting position. His eyes remained closed, the left one swollen shut. The three of them sat motionless, listening hard.

"We don't need some know-it-all sticking his nose into our business."

"We're doing what's legally right."

"Yeah!"

"Stop for a moment and consider the Golden Rule, to do unto others as you would want done to you, to live a life of kindness and consideration." Noah Pemberton continued, his voice rising dramatically, "There is a door open for thee, following in the footsteps of goodness, through the dark pathway of evil, into the light."

Flower stood at the bars, looked out of the cell, and peered at the doorway beside the cupboard; it was slightly ajar, and there was darkness in the passageway beyond. Eldon followed her glance. The marshal and his deputy slept on. Cleo started to rock again, then stopped.

"You're interfering with our business. You've no right. The marshal's here to make sure things are done true to the law of the land."

"You can follow a larger law, a law that follows the path of morality. There will come a time when you must answer to a higher power. What will that answer be?"

"You can be a righteous person and still have slaves."

"I think not." Now there was silence. "There is a key to the kingdom of heaven, and that key lies within every human heart. That is my message. The key is the instrument to free you from the burden of sin; it opens the door to the passage, leading to salvation."

Flower brought her hand from her apron pocket and held up the key for her father to see.

CHAPTER 42
Felicia

ASHLEY ARRIVED late to the lunchtime rehearsal. She swept into the auditorium and up onto center stage. Mr. Butler's head swung around looking for Josh.

"We still have time for the Thanksgiving duet. Where's Mayor Thomas?"

"Sorry, gotta go," answered Josh. "I promised Miss Peabody I'd help set up a science experiment for our class."

"That's just an excuse," said Ashley. "He never wants to practice."

"Who's been here for twenty minutes already?" asked Josh.

Mr. Butler intervened. "Come now. It only takes three minutes. Let's have a quick run-through."

Josh reluctantly left his group of friends. "Don't listen," he muttered to them as he walked by. On stage, he stood with seeming indifference beside Ashley. Mr. Butler counted, "A one and a two...," and the pair began to sing. Josh's effort was calm and straightforward; in contrast,

Ashley "emoted" with gusto. As they finished the song, she opened her arms wide and accidentally whacked Josh in the chest. He staggered back and clutched his shirt.

Mr. Butler glowered. "This is not a comedy. It's a serious effort to bring to life our historical heritage. And furthermore, we present this play in two weeks, just before the holidays. There's no time for foolishness. Do I make myself clear?"

"It's Josh that's being gross, not me," said Ashley.

"Gotta go," Josh said, as he bounded down the steps of the stage, up the aisle, and out into the hall.

"Are the four singing pioneer women ready?" shouted Mr. Butler.

"That's us. We're up," said Renate.

"Let's go, pioneer women," said Dodie.

"I don't feel like a pioneer woman," said Felicia.

"You don't look like one, either," said Ashley, as she took a seat.

"What did she say?" asked Sophie.

"She said I don't look like a pioneer woman."

"That's probably a good thing."

The four girls stepped onto the stage. Mr. Butler pointed out the marks on the floor. "Look for these white stars. They tell you where to stand. Mrs. Brody is going to accompany you. We'll have a full rehearsal next week." Mr. Butler turned to the piano player who raised her hands over the keyboard and, at his signal, began to pound out the music. The girls sang along.

After, they sat with their sandwiches and watched the rehearsal proceed.

"Matt is a natural as the parson."

"You can tell, though, he's just bursting to say something funny."

"Poor Josh has to sing with Ashley."

"I'd rather have the flu."

Delia and Florence sat after supper and sipped their tea. Felicia brought books to the table.

"Ready to start your homework?"

"I've been reading these books Mr. Allenby gave me. Thought I'd let you have a look at them before I take them back to the library."

"What are they about?"

"The Underground Railroad."

"Interesting?"

"Very. Here's one on quilts, Nana."

"Oh, let me see that. I used to enjoy stitching before my fingers got old."

"There's a theory that they used quilts to signal each other," said Felicia. "They'd hang them over a fence or something, and the people who were running away got the message."

"What message?"

"There were a lot of different messages, I guess." Felicia flipped through the illustrations. "They think different patterns meant different things. This one's called the 'monkey wrench'—it meant get organized with the tools you'll need. This one is a wagon wheel. That's obvious. My favorite is the 'bear's paw.' They were supposed to follow the bear's paw print in the ground 'cause the bear would find water to drink and berries to eat."

"I'm not sure I'd want to follow a bear," said Delia.

Felicia turned another page. "This is so pretty, the star. You know they were supposed to follow the North Star. I looked up at the sky the other night, and I couldn't tell which one was which. I don't know how they did."

"Practice, I guess."

"It was dangerous," said Florence. You could go to jail, or worse, for helping a slave escape. You'd have to be a really strong person to do that."

"Except look at this." Flower picked up another book and leafed through until she found the page she wanted. "Here's a lady called Harriet Tubman. She helped hundreds of people escape."

"Right, I know all about her. And she was no bigger than a minute, you know," said Florence.

"Exactly. And, this is kind of funny, it shows how tough she was. She was taking these people north, and one person got scared and said he was going to go back to the plantation where he was a slave."

"Changed his mind," said Delia.

"So this little Harriet—" Felicia started to laugh. "I can just picture it. She takes out her gun and says, 'Dead men don't talk.' She's going to shoot him unless he keeps going, so he does."

Florence shook her head.

Delia said, "I can picture the drama of the escape, but then what happened when they got here? What did they do?"

"The book talks about two settlements," said Felicia. "One was called the Elgin and the other was the Dawn. They both had schools for the children, and the adults were taught how to do things. One had a sawmill and a gristmill. What's that?"

"That's where they ground up grain," said Delia.

"Nana, I was wondering."

"Yes, dear."

"Do you think our family, early on, might have lived in one of those settlements? You said someone was a blacksmith and someone else made furniture. Do you think they might have learned how to do that in one of those places?"

"Might have. Of course, I have no way of knowing for sure. You're talking about a long time ago."

"I wonder," said Felicia, "what happened to those communities? Where did the people go?"

"People usually don't stay in one place," said Delia. "They look for work or schooling. Cities are a draw. Most of them must have moved on. Lord knows where you'll live when you're grown up."

"I hope I'll be close enough to you and Nana so we can still see each other."

"I hope so too."

"So many separations." Florence sighed. "Hold fast to your family. If you learn one thing from all this reading, it should be that. Loyalty to each other is the mainstay of our heritage."

CHAPTER 43
Flower

NOAH PEMBERTON'S voice continued, insistent, hectoring, and urgent, riding up and down on opposing waves of persuasion and condemnation. The marshal and his deputy still slept soundly.

Flower held up the key, motioned for her father to come to the cell door. He struggled to his feet, holding on to her shoulder. Flower pointed at the far door with the dark hallway beyond. She reached through the bars, lengthening her arm as far as she could, then bending it at the elbow so that the key could be brought toward the opening of the lock. She couldn't see properly to insert it, so she thrust her other hand through to touch the outline where the key should fit. Her fingers felt stiff and awkward with nervousness, and, with a sudden clatter, the key dropped to the floor.

The lawmen slept on. The key lay on the floor, too far away for Flower to reach it. Eldon's large arm would not fit through the bars. He motioned for Cleo, who knelt down and stretched to retrieve it. She tried to place the key in the lock, but her arm was too long and the angle was awkward, so she handed the key back to her daughter. Flower took a deep breath and tried again. This time, with a scrape and a click, the key turned in its slot, and the door opened.

Flower led the way. On tiptoe, they left the cell, creeping past the men sleeping at the desk, through the doorway, into the dark hall. Her mother eased the door shut behind them. They descended down and down, the hall becoming a tunnel. There was no light, only inky blackness. Flower held her fingertips against the damp, stony wall for guidance. Something squeaked and scampered past her feet. She flinched but kept going, her father's hand on her shoulder.

Just when she thought there was no end to this journey, Flower saw a faint trace of light ahead, outlining the base of a doorway. The family bumped into each other as they came to a stop before it. They could hear Noah's voice once more, although they couldn't make out what he was saying.

Her father's hands brushed against the door, but it was Flower's hand that found the handle. The latch lifted and the door creaked open, letting in a sliver of light. She peered out from behind its edge. There was no angry mob, just a wagon with a tethered horse standing sleepily, slack reins held by the driver. He turned his head at the sound and looked straight at her. She shrank from his burning gaze, closed the door, and slid the latch back into place.

Almost immediately, there was a rap on the other side of the door. "Come quickly, there's little time."

"Pa?"

"Open the door," said Eldon.

Flower swallowed and did as her father instructed.

A man stood before her, his hat tilted low over his dark face. "Follow me." When they hesitated, he said, "Don't dawdle!" The voice was quiet but insistent. They were led to the back of the wagon. The driver lifted a blanket and swiftly moved two large boxes. Eldon, Cleo, and their baby were directed into the spaces, then covered with the blanket.

Flower was hoisted up onto the seat beside the driver. He reached behind him and presented her with a bonnet. "Put this on."

The ribbons slid through her fingers. "I don't know how."

He released the reins and jammed the hat onto her head, tying the bow roughly under her chin. "Look down," he commanded, as he clucked the horse forward. They made their way around from the back to the front of the jailhouse, through a sea of men. A fist pounded the sides of the passing wagon. Flower concentrated on keeping her face down and hidden. Staring at her lap, she noticed her brown hands and drew them up into her sleeves.

Noah's voice soared over their heads, as if heralding their escape. "Redemption is at hand for those who follow in the footsteps of the good and the righteous."

Less respectful voices grumbled. "Go follow your own footsteps."

"Yeah, straight to hell."

Torches flamed in the darkness, reminding Flower of the night she and her family had survived the river crossing, how they had sat around the fire trying to keep warm. Then Noah Pemberton had appeared suddenly before them, his face like a visiting ghost in the flickering light.

Now his voice soared over the mob. "Shame! The shame of slavery casts its shadow on so many."

Though she didn't look up, she could picture that face and knew that he was providing a majestic vision to this crowd, few of whom dared to contradict him. As they made their way out of town, his voice softened and receded. He might have been comforting the crowd that he had so chastised, but Flower thought that the words were especially meant for her to hear.

"Bless you...."

CHAPTER 44
Felicia

MISS PEABODY LEANED over her desk and checked a list. "Ashley, are you ready to give your presentation?"

"I guess so. I need a minute to go change."

"Change?"

"Yes."

"Well, all right, but don't be too long, please." The teacher sat at her desk, looked up at the clock, and shuffled papers impatiently.

Ashley returned wearing a rose silk gown, the flounced skirt brushing the floor. She lifted the skirt a few inches and turned in a pirouette. "Isn't this dress beautiful? It belonged to my great-great-great-great-aunt. She wore it to special functions."

"It's so pretty. Can I touch it?" asked Lucy.

Ashley took a step backward. "Of course not. It's too precious." The class was silent. Ashley continued, "She had a huge wardrobe, with many, many beautiful clothes: dresses, hats with feathers and ribbons, beaded handbags—"

"Is that it?" asked Matt.

"Is that what?" countered Ashley.

"Your presentation—a closet list?"

"Hardly."

"Please don't interrupt, Matt. Continue, Ashley," said Miss Peabody.

"My mother's family came from Virginia. They had this big, beautiful house that they lived in, with pillars right up to the roof and flowers everywhere. They also had a huge plantation where they grew cotton. They had lots of slaves to pick the cotton and do the work." Ashley drawled on the word *slaves* and Felicia felt as if a spotlight had positioned itself right above her head.

"This project is meant to focus on our Canadian heritage," emphasized Miss Peabody. "Perhaps you should skip forward a generation or two."

"They came to Canada when the Americans got into a fight with the British."

"Ah, yes, the American Revolution," said the teacher. "Your family was loyal to the Crown of England."

"Yes, they were United Empire Loyalists. And I think they were friends with the king," said Ashley.

"Can you describe what life was like for them during this period?"

Ashley held up a piece of paper. "My grandma said

I could bring this letter to class. It's one written by my great-great-great—"

"Yes, how interesting. What does she say?"

"She was writing to her sister. 'Yesterday and today, feeling better, enjoyed a rest beneath the garden tree, shaded and cool. The maid there came to me to announce the visitation of the Farrow cousins. We supped tea and shared civil discourse.' The Farrows were very important people. My family knew a lot of important people. They were invited to fancy dress balls and parties. When my family arrived in Canada, they built another beautiful house. They brought lots of their things with them, even their slaves. They were good to their slaves, and they let them be servants."

Sophie said, "Maybe the slaves didn't want to be servants. Maybe they just wanted to be free."

"They were free, but they needed to be looked after, so my family kept them and looked after them."

"Excuse me." Felicia was on her feet. She hesitated with all eyes upon her but then said, "I think you're wrong, Ashley."

"What about?"

"They didn't need to be 'looked after.' You think that every black person was a slave or a servant, but that's not true. There's a whole history you don't know about."

"Oh really."

"Yes. Many slaves ran away. They didn't all make it,

but some of them did; and some of them lived around here. And they weren't all servants. They taught school and made furniture. They farmed, and they were fishermen." Felicia started to feel short of breath, but she persisted. "They ran companies, and they were soldiers. There were even two newspapers."

Miss Peabody said, "Thank you, Felicia. That thoughtful response is a good prelude to my announcement." The class was silently expectant. "Mr. Allenby and I find this part of our history very interesting. We've organized a field trip for next week to a museum that documents the settlement of escaped slaves in the surrounding area; it's just outside of Collingwood." She turned to a pile of papers on her desk and started to hand them out. "These are the permission forms. Please take them home to be signed."

As if suddenly remembering her other student, the teacher turned and said, "Oh, Ashley. Are you finished your presentation?" Ashley nodded. "Class, does anyone have questions for Ashley?"

Ashley looked out at her classmates, but there were no questions and no one said anything; so scrunching her flowered skirt with both fists, she turned and walked through the doorway and out of the classroom.

And for one brief micro millisecond, Felicia felt pity for Ashley.

CHAPTER 45
Flower

THE FAMILY TRAVELED throughout the night. Flower sat nodding with exhaustion beside the driver. As the sun began to warm the sky, they stopped in front of a farmhouse. A quilt lay displayed over the verandah railing. It was blue and green with a white star in the center.

"This here's the first stop. Down you get."

"Can I take this hat off now?"

"Yes."

"It's tied so I can't do it."

"Just pull on the ribbon, you foolish girl."

Flower pulled, and the tie came loose. She placed the bonnet on the bench and then slid down from her perch, clipping her chin on the side of the wagon. She didn't cry out, though it hurt; she stood rubbing it as she watched the driver remove the blanket and box tops so that her parents could leave their hiding place.

"Can you stand?" the driver asked.

"I think so." Eldon winced with pain as he stretched

his legs onto the ground. Cleo struggled out and leaned against him, her eyes clamped shut. Gabriel was wrapped against her body.

"We've got a ways to go yet. Hold on, here comes Jake."

They turned to see a tall man coming down the porch steps. Flower was surprised to see his skin was brown, just like hers.

He moved rapidly, with long, healthy strides. "You've got a wagonful!"

"A whole family: ma and pa, a girl child, and a babe."

"Able to travel on foot?"

"We've been doing it," said Eldon. "Do we have far yet?"

"Enough." He looked at Cleo. "How about the woman?"

"She's able. She's been walking, haven't you?" Eldon looked at his wife. When she didn't respond, he nudged her. "You're able, aren't you?" Cleo slowly opened her eyes and stared vacantly ahead. "See, she's able."

Jake and the driver exchanged glances. "I don't know. She doesn't look good."

"I'll help her," said Flower. She stood beside her mother. "I'll take the baby." The cocooned infant was transferred to her.

"Options are few," said Jake. "We'd best keep moving."

The driver stepped up to his seat on the wagon and

snapped the reins. The wheels started to turn. Jake waved good-bye to him and to a woman standing on the porch. She folded the quilt and returned his wave. The family followed Jake as he walked into the trees.

They walked for four hours, stopping every hour to rest. When the sun was high, they sat by a brook and drank from its icy water. Jake pulled bread and cheese from a sack. Flower's stomach reacted with punishing spasms as she pushed the food into her mouth. She was so hungry, she hardly took the time to chew it.

She tore the bread into tiny bits for Gabriel, slid cupped water into his mouth.

Eldon fed Cleo and spoke encouragingly to her, as Flower did to Gabriel. "Come on now, take a little bit."

"Don't *you* forget to eat, Pa."

"I know."

"We have to keep strong."

"I know, daughter."

Walking became agony for the last hour. Cleo could barely lift her feet; she was supported, one on each side, by her daughter and limping husband. Flower was ready to cry out "enough!" when Jake halted ahead of her, his hand raised. They waited in a grove of shrubs while he continued ahead. Flower lost sight of him, but she could see a small cabin amid many trees as she peered through the thicket of low-lying branches.

"All clear." He led them to a log building with a dirt floor and no windows, just a door. There was a heap of hay in one corner. Eldon eased Cleo onto it, then released Gabriel from his sling and laid him alongside his mother. Flower wanted to lie down, too, but stood and waited.

"It's not much, but it's safe, for the time being anyhow," said Jake.

Eldon said, "We're thankful for your help. You saved our lives. If only there was some way to repay you…"

Jake waved the words away with his hand. "We have to help each other. I'm leaving you bread, cheese, and some salt pork. Should last for about three days. There's a stream near here for your drinking needs."

"Thank you."

"When you're ready, follow the stream north to the Buxton place, about a day's walk from here. If it's safe, they'll have the quilt out."

Jake disappeared into the trees. They were alone. Flower watched her father sink to the ground beside Cleo and the baby. Her parents fell asleep immediately, but Gabriel started to cry weakly. She picked him up and carried him outside into the fading sunlight.

"Let's get us a drink."

The sound of the flowing water made the stream easy to find. Flower set her little brother on the ground, cupped water for herself, and drank greedily, then offered it to Gabriel.

"That's good. You're learning to drink like a big boy," she said, as he sucked the water out of her palm. "Let's go back and have some more bread."

Flower tried to wake her mother and father. She knew it was important for them to eat and drink, but Eldon didn't respond to her urgings, and Cleo only whimpered and curled up on her side. Flower lay down with Gabriel between herself and her mother, and she fell into an exhausted sleep.

"Help me! Help me! God help me!"

Flower jumped awake at the sound of her mother's cries. Moonlight flooded through the open door into the interior of the cabin. She could see Cleo pulling at her chest. "Ma! What's wrong?"

"Get it off me! Help me!"

"Get what off you?" Eldon was barely awake.

"The snake! There's a snake! Get it off me! Oh, please get it off me!"

"Ma, you're dreaming, there's no snake."

"The snake! The snake! Get it off of me! Oh, please…"

Flower put her hand on her mother's chest. "There. I've got it. I took it off you. It's all gone now."

"It's gone?"

"Yes. It's gone. It's never coming back."

"Thank you."

Flower transferred her hand to her mother's face. The skin was burning hot and her breath was rapid. Flower could see the pulse beating in her neck. "Pa, she's got a fever, she's sick." Eldon didn't answer. He was asleep again, snoring. Flower felt his forehead. It was also hot.

For the next three days, Flower cared for her family. She fed them by hand. She carried water from the stream and forced them to drink. She dipped Cleo's shawl in the water and used the wet cloth to bathe and cool their feverish faces. She sang to her brother, fed him and played with him, and worried about when her family would be well enough to continue their journey.

CHAPTER 46
Felicia

THE REHEARSAL came to a disorganized halt with Mr. Butler waving his script in the air. "Quiet, please. Quiet, please." His face reddened with the effort of raising his voice, and he tugged at his hair with frustration. It stood up from his head in gray wiry spokes surrounding the gleam of a bald center. "We've still got some fine-tuning to do with this production. I want everyone to be prepared to work harder at tomorrow's rehearsal."

There were a few yes sirs and okays as the students made their way out of the auditorium.

Dodie asked, "What do you think we should wear for this thing?"

"I think we should all wear black."

Mr. Butler overheard them. "You may be wondering about costumes. For the boys, dark clothes if possible; for the girls, dresses or skirts, perhaps flowered. A parents' group has volunteered to sew white aprons for all of the girls to wear as well."

"Except for me," said Ashley.

"I have this beautiful dress—" began Renate.

"I have this beautiful dress that's been in my family for ages. I'm going to wear it," said Ashley.

"That will be fine," said Mr. Butler. "Oh, by the way, I should tell you we have a sold out show! What do you think of that?"

The group applauded. "Okay, everyone. We'll break early today—there seems to be a problem with focus—but I want to see everyone again tomorrow after school for a full run-through of the show."

Matt and Josh joined the girls as they walked to the cafeteria. "Maybe we'll get a TV series out of this," said Matt.

"Little Nerds on the Prairie?" asked Josh. "I can't believe how humiliating this is! You guys don't understand. If only I could weasel my way out of it. I'm tempted to say I've sprained my ankle or something."

"It's only for one night," said Sophie.

"One night of horror."

"I think Ashley's getting a big crush on you."

"Please!"

"It's tough being the star of the show," said Dodie.

"You think it's funny, but it isn't. The whole school and their families will be there, all laughing at me."

"Nobody will be laughing at you." Felicia said.

"And not everyone's family will be there," said Sophie. "My dad's going to be away, and my mom can't get a baby-sitter for my little brother."

"My aunt and two of my friends will be visiting from the city. They're coming with my mom and grandma," said Felicia.

"Will they all be in the front row?"

"I hope not!"

"I bet they'll be in the front row," Josh said. "With a camera."

Felicia felt a quiver of embarrassment at the thought. She wondered if Lenore and Rosalee would find the production a silly waste of time. Lost in thought, she didn't immediately notice Ashley, who was waiting at her locker.

Felicia moaned inwardly, but said nothing.

Ashley's voice was hot with rage. "Here she is. Little Miss Know-It-All. You think you're so smart, don't you?"

Felicia didn't say anything, so Ashley continued. "Ruining my project with your little sermon, being such a sucky toad to Miss Peabody."

"Sticks and stones, Ashley. Bad names can't hurt me. You're just embarrassed because your presentation was so lame. And you'd love it to be somebody else's fault."

"You just wait. You're in for a rude surprise. You think you're so smart. You may have a little trouble in the future."

Felicia shook her head. "I'd like to open my locker."

Ashley stepped aside. "You just wait." Felicia watched her disappear in the throng of students.

When Felicia got to the cafeteria, she found Dodie, Sophie, Renate, Josh, and Matt engaged in the daily routine of displaying their lunches and trading for something they liked better.

"Guys, Ashley just told me that something bad is going to happen to me. 'Just wait,' she said."

"What's she going to do?" asked Matt. "Trip you off the stage?"

"I don't know."

Melissa walked over to the table with a whole tin of marshmallow squares. "These are for everybody. They're left over from my mom's coffee party. She says she wants them out of the house so she won't eat them."

The squares were passed around. When they arrived in Felicia's hand, she hesitated, remembering Melissa's participation in the washroom bullying.

"Please take one, Felicia." Melissa smiled in a warm and special way, and Felicia understood that she wanted to move on from that nasty incident.

Felicia took a square and bit into it, hoping it wouldn't blow up in her face as a nasty joke. It was gooey and delicious. "Thank you."

A scrunched-up lunch bag bounced off Melissa's head and landed on the table.

"Ashley's mad at me," said Melissa. "She's mad at Lucy too."

They all looked at the table behind them where Ashley sat with her diminished posse of two people.

"Why is she mad at you and Lucy?" Sophie asked.

"We stopped listening to her. Her constant mean attitude just got boring, such a drag. Everything was always bad, bad, bad. Especially all the stuff about Felicia. She was telling everyone she could that Felicia's family had been in trouble in the city. She said that's why you had to move. She said Felicia's dad was in jail."

"That is so not true," said Felicia.

"We figured that out when the story got wilder and wilder. She said you had an uncle who was a terrorist."

They all burst into spontaneous laughter. "Oh Felicia," said Matt, "you are so scary."

Only Felicia was solemn. "That is just crazy."

"We know. We told her, and now she's not speaking to us."

"Ashley's always mad at somebody," said Renate, trying to comfort Felicia.

"But especially me," said Felicia. "She hates me. She can't stand the sight of me, and I know why, but I can't do anything about it."

"What do you mean?"

"It's because I'm not white." The group was silent as Felicia gathered the courage to continue. "But I like the color of my skin."

"Why wouldn't you?" asked Josh.

Felicia smiled at Josh. "Some people don't like it." She glanced at Melissa, then looked down at her lap. "They keep telling me that I don't fit in here because I look different."

"We're all of us different," said Dodie, "in one way or another."

"The color of my skin is separated into millions of freckles," said Sophie. "I get teased about it all the time."

Felicia smiled at Sophie's dappled face. "I think you look neat, especially your eyes—sometimes they look gray, and sometimes they look green."

"Thank you."

"Well, it's true what people say," said Renate, "it's the spirit inside us that really counts—and how we treat each other."

CHAPTER 47
Flower

ON THE FOURTH morning, Flower could see her breath in the air and was amazed at the sight of white powder on the ground. She wrapped her mother's cloak tightly around herself, enclosing Gabriel in its warmth as she made her way to the stream. Crusts of patterned crystal rimmed the rocky edges, but the water flowed freely.

By midmorning, the snow was gone. Eldon came out of the cabin, stood absorbing the sunlight. He said to Flower, "The weather is changing. The more we travel north, the colder it's going to get. Time to get a move on."

"What about Ma? Can she do it?"

They both looked in at Cleo curled up on the hay. Eldon said, "Come, Cleo, try to get yourself moving. We can't stay here forever." Cleo didn't answer. Eldon raised his voice. "You've got to try!" His words disappeared in the midst of a barking cough. He pressed his hand against his chest.

"I'm trying." Cleo struggled to sit. She looked up at

her daughter. "How's my darlin' doing? Working so hard for us."

"Can you get up? Can you walk a little bit to the water?"

"I think so." Cleo took hold of Eldon's hand. He pulled. "Ow! Easy, easy." Another gentler tug, and she was on her feet. She swayed and closed her eyes. "Oh, my head's spinning."

"Come on out into the sun. It feels good and warm."

Cleo took wobbly steps outside and stood leaning against the cabin. "That does feel good."

Flower said, "You both have to start walking. We'll run out of food soon."

"And the northern weather is on our doorstep," added Eldon.

Cleo's legs buckled, and she sank to the ground in a heap. "I don't think I can do it. You two carry on without me."

"Don't talk foolish." Eldon knelt weakly beside his wife and frowned. "I'm a burden now too." He looked up at Flower. "You feeling all right?"

"Yes."

"Truthfully?"

"Yes, Pa."

"Think you can follow that stream if I send you in the right direction?"

"By myself?"

"Yes."

"I don't know. I don't want to be by myself."

"It's the only way for now. Your ma and I can't make it."

"I don't want to leave you. I don't want to be all alone."

"We need you to do it, daughter, to find these Buxton people. It's not far. Go find help and bring it back to us."

Flower's throat began to ache. "I don't want to leave you." She pressed her teary face against her mother's hand.

"It's the only way."

Cleo helped Flower measure out some of the remaining bread and meat and pack it into a cloth square. They held each other close, then Flower kissed Gabriel and walked with her father to the stream. Together they studied the place of the sun in the sky and determined which way was north. Eldon patted her on the back, and pushed her gently forward. "You be on your way now."

Flower started walking and didn't look back. She placed one foot in front of the other and willed her mind to be blank. She didn't want to think about losing her mother and father. Would they really recover and join her again? She didn't want to think about Gabriel, the warmth of his round body when she carried him, the way he held his arms out to her when he wanted to be picked up. She didn't want to think about wicked slave catchers, howling dogs, or any wild creatures: bears, snakes, or mountain lions. She plodded along for hours until her mouth was dry and her legs were aching, then sat on a stone near the brook and rested.

When she knelt down to drink from the flowing water, Flower heard a sound. She lifted her head, the water dripping out of her mouth and back into the stream. It wasn't a bird. It was a person, whistling. Flower got to her feet. She had to hide. Where? There were no bushes to crouch behind, only trees. She remembered her father climbing one and made a panicked decision to do the same. It wasn't easy—her feet scuffed and slid, and the branches scratched her face and hurt her hands. She settled on a limb, leaned against the trunk, and tried to breathe without making a sound. The whistling stopped. Flower knew that the person had heard her and was listening too.

There was quiet, then soft footsteps. Flower held her breath, grasped the tree with desperation. The branch she was standing on moved up and down with her weight.

"Those branches are moving mighty hard. Not much breeze. Maybe a cougar, or someone hiding in a difficult spot."

Flower pressed her forehead against the rough bark. One foot started to slip.

"If you're a friend, I'm a friend too. If you're here to cause harm, I have a gun, and I know how to use it."

A metallic click signaled the release of a bolt, and

Flower imagined a gun barrel aimed straight up at her. She shook with fear, losing her foothold. She tried to cling with her hands and arms, but couldn't manage. The branches thwacked her legs as she scratched and scraped her way down, landing in a painful clump at the base of the tree.

Footsteps approached. Flower kept her face hidden. "Please don't shoot me."

"I know how to use it, but I don't like to use it. What's your name, and what were you doing in the tree?"

Flower looked at his muddy boots. "I heard you coming."

"Hiding from me? No need to. Get up now and let me see you." He reached down as he spoke and, grasping an arm, tugged her to her feet. Flower backed away, stared at the gloved hand holding the gun, not daring to look at the stranger's face.

"I always carry it. You never know what's around the corner. What's your name?"

"Flower."

"A pretty name for a pretty little girl. Where's your kin?"

Flower didn't want to reveal her family's hiding place. She wasn't sure she could trust this person, though he sounded kind.

"Where you headed then?"

Flower finally found the courage to look up, to see her

inquisitor's face. Her eyes widened with surprise. His skin was darker than Jake's.

"I'm following the stream north to the Buxton place. If the quilt is out, it's safe."

"You would be right about that." He smiled at her and extended his hand. "I'm Abe Buxton. Pleased to make your acquaintance."

CHAPTER 48
Felicia

"I WANT YOU in groups of four," said Miss Peabody. "You have to share."

Felicia, Renate, Sophie, and Dodie automatically formed their own foursome and stood expectantly in front of a microscope.

"What are we going to look at?"

The teacher opened a large plastic container. "We're going to study a form of flatworm called Planaria. They're most interesting, because—"

"WORMS!"

"Remember, everyone, you're on your way to adulthood."

"Some have a longer way to go," said Matt.

Miss Peabody continued, "Each foursome will receive one. Once you have yours, place it on the glass provided and look at it under the microscope."

"How are we going to pick them up?" asked Renate.

"Very carefully," said Matt.

"With tweezers. There's nothing to it," said the teacher.

"We might hurt them."

"Please, Sophie," said Dodie.

"As you examine them, I'd like you to make notes," continued Miss Peabody. "After that, you'll be given a scalpel, and I want you to cut them in half."

The classroom erupted. Miss Peabody raised her hands for quiet. "The reason these creatures are used in research is because they have the amazing ability to regenerate themselves."

"Let's do it," said Dodie, picking up a pair of tweezers. She grasped the tiny creature and placed it on a glass slide, slid it under the microscope, and peered down. "It's cute!"

Later, at the stable, they were still talking about the worm as they groomed their horses.

"It was sweet. I didn't expect it to have those big eyes looking up at us."

"Good-looking, for a worm," agreed Felicia.

Sophie asked, "How do we know for sure it doesn't feel pain?"

"'Cause it's a worm. It doesn't feel anything."

"Dodie, sometimes it sounds as if you think you know everything, and you don't," said Sophie.

"Sometimes we just look at things differently," said Felicia. She bent to lift a hoof, pick in hand, but Star stood firm and refused to release her foot. "Come on, give me your hoof." Felicia tugged, but the horse didn't move. Lift your foot! How can I clean it?"

Their instructor came out of the tack room. "Anything wrong?"

"Star is being stubborn or lazy or something. She won't lift her foot."

"Let me see." Francine ran her hand down the front left leg and asked, "Can you give me your foot, good girl? No? Let's try another one." She had the horse lift the other front foot. "Here's the trouble." Her strong fingers pried out a stone lodged inside the rim of the metal shoe. "She didn't want to put her weight on this foot. It hurt." Francine scraped away a bit of dirt.

Felicia felt hot with shame. "I'm sorry. I always start with the front left. I didn't mean to hurt her."

"Don't worry about it. She's fine. It's a lesson learned for you. The horse can't tell you what's wrong. You have to search it out."

"Poor Star. I feel terrible. I never want you to be hurt."

"Forget about it. She has." Francine patted her student on the back.

The horse seemed unaffected by the incident, trotting and cantering with ease, but the episode remained in Felicia's mind.

Later at the dinner table, Felicia talked to her family about the incident. "I felt so bad. She's such a big animal, but she depends on someone like me to look after her."

"I guess years ago they roamed free, in herds, but they had to look out for wild animals that could attack them," said Florence.

"Rufus depends on us too," said Felicia.

"That cat is getting cheeky." Delia shushed him away from the table. "He keeps trying to climb in my lap while I'm eating!"

"He's just been fed." They glanced at the bowl of untouched kibble on the floor. "Guess he prefers the salmon cakes we're having."

"What did you do in school today?" Florence asked.

"Science. We had to look at this weird worm under the microscope and then cut it in half. The teacher says it's an interesting worm 'cause it can grow itself back."

"That so?"

"And, if you think I'm caring too much about Star, you should have heard Sophie with the worm. She worried it was hurt."

"Sophie is one sensitive soul."

CHAPTER 49
Flower

A WOMAN STOOD on the porch. "Abe, is that you?"

"Yep, and I've got someone with me."

Flower was introduced to Abe's sister, Abigail, a stout, slow-moving woman. Her face was broad and kindly, with eyes that were milky and stared off into the distance rather than at Flower.

"Where you from, child?"

"A long ways away." Flower was still reluctant to give information. The world was a dangerous place.

"Have you been traveling on your own all this time?"

"Her kin's up in the hills. Feeling poorly. I'll see to them tomorrow," said Abe.

"Tomorrow? They're all alone and sick, and they don't have me to look after them."

"I don't like to travel at night. Some of the big animals hunt then, and I don't want to be their dinner. I'll leave first thing in the morning and bring your folks back good and early."

"Thank you."

"You must be wanting some supper," said Abigail.

"Yes, please." Flower followed Abigail inside and sat at the table. She watched as Abigail made her way in the small space without walking into anything.

Abe explained, "Abigail has trouble seeing things, but she manages real well; and she's a fine cook, as you're about to learn." Supper was vegetable soup. After bolting her small meal, Flower nursed her scalded tongue. She could feel a blister forming.

"Where you headed now?"

"I don't know."

"How long have you been traveling?"

"A while."

"Feeling fearful? Had some bad times?" Flower lowered her head and studied the worn tabletop, willing herself not to cry. "You're in safe hands now, for the time being, anyway."

At dusk, Flower was instructed to sleep at the foot of Abigail's bed. She was shown a hiding place under the floorboards beneath the bed. "As soon as I tell you, you get down there quick, you hear?"

"Tonight?"

"We never know. We are always ready for anything."

The next morning, Abe left just as the sun crested the horizon. Flower stood in the doorway and watched him disappear into the trees. The day was a long wait for her. She chopped carrots and turnips, swept the cabin, and watched as Abigail pummeled dough to make bread. It was late afternoon when Flower heard the sound of hooves trudging softly through grass. Abe led his horse, which walked with a steady, loping gait. Cleo sat on top and swayed with each step. Eldon walked alongside. Flower ran out to greet them, hugged her father, and then lifted the baby out of her mother's lap. "You're here! You're here!"

Abigail made them welcome and ushered them into the cabin where they sat around the table and ate the soup and freshly baked bread. Eldon and Cleo looked hollow-eyed and exhausted in the dimming light, while Gabriel nestled once more in his sister's lap.

"This soup tastes like it's come straight from heaven," said Cleo.

"Just some vegetables, late ones from the garden."

"The heavenly garden."

"How can you live here without being bothered, as we are?" asked Eldon. "And that Jake fellow too?"

"Jake was able to buy his freedom. My master died some years ago. Left a will, written up for them in charge to see and read. Said I was a free man, my sister too. We found our way to this place, just outside of Ripley, built our house, and here we are."

"And no one's come after you?"

"No. Not that we rest easy. I'm thinking we're not worth much. We're getting on in age, and Abigail's got the blindness. For you folks, it's different. Your master wants you back, you and your kin."

"He's not going to get us back."

"You folks are spent," said Abe.

"We truly are."

"And more miles to travel."

"We pray we have the strength," said Cleo.

"You'd best rest here for a day or two. Do you know how to get where you're going?"

"Bits and pieces."

"That's no good. I'll tell you what I'm going to do. I'm going to make my way to the next station in the morning and send on a message. You need a guiding hand."

Abe was gone for two days. The family waited and rested, always with an ear for men's voices or dogs barking. Cleo felt well enough to help Abigail in the kitchen, while Flower tended to her little brother.

At dusk on the second day, they heard a bird cry, three distinct notes. "That'll be Abe." Abigail whistled in return, and, in a few minutes, he joined them on the porch. He was carrying two rabbits, their lifeless bodies slung over his shoulder.

"Here I am, and with supper too."

"We've had our meal. There's some saved for you."

"This is for the next one, then. We'll be sharing it with others."

The next day they set out again. Abe led the horse; Cleo riding it. Flower walked beside her father, sometimes carrying Gabriel. After four hours, they approached a log house with smoke curling up from the chimney.

A man and a woman came out to greet them. "Come on up to the porch. No sense standing here visiting in the yard."

They were ushered up the steps as Abe led the horse to a fenced pasture. "Come and meet Hazel. She's going to be your guiding angel, leading you to the Promised Land." Flower frowned with disappointment. She had pictured a big, strong man like her father, someone brave and invincible, someone capable of protecting them. Instead, a small black woman stared back at them, plain faced and ordinary.

CHAPTER 50
Felicia

FELICIA PEERED out between curtain folds. Behind her was backstage bedlam. She watched the audience file into the auditorium, saw her family and friends fill the front row. Josh's prediction was correct. Delia lifted a camera and focused.

"My mom's in the front row with a camera."

"Better not screw up then."

"Thanks. Now I'm really nervous."

Delia waved. Felicia returned the wave and abruptly closed the curtain. "Renate, you look weird with those penciled-on freckles."

"You look pretty funny, too, in that bonnet."

"My stomach feels funny. Is that what they mean by butterflies?"

"Probably. Come and help us with Sophie. She's bawling and ruining her makeup. It's running all down her face."

They found Dodie and Sophie in the library behind a bookshelf. Sophie's eyes were red-rimmed and teary.

Blackened rivulets streaked her rosy cheeks. She blew her nose.

"You sound like a fog horn."

Sophie tried to smile, but her mouth collapsed. "I hate this!"

"Come on, it's going to be fun," said Dodie.

"It is not! It's your idea of fun, not mine."

"Well, we're signed up, and we've been rehearsing for ages, and now it's time to do it."

"We'll be with you." Renate took Sophie's hand.

"We'll all stand together," said Felicia. "We can stand a bit in front of you, if you want."

"Maybe."

"Let's find Melissa's mom. She'll fix your makeup." They walked back into their classroom where parent volunteers were applying makeup and adjusting costumes. A pencil and brush restored Sophie's face.

Sandy, the stage manager, poked her head in the doorway. "Five minutes to curtain. Everyone in your places, please." Felicia felt her heartbeat quicken, squeezed Sophie's hand. The four girls left the classroom and stationed themselves in the wings, listening as Mr. Butler introduced himself and talked about the theme of the play. Then the pianist started to play the opening theme.

The production passed in a brilliant haze of light and color. At the end of the first act, Matt's beard came loose and began to flap on one side of his face when he spoke. He turned and presented his good side to the audience until his scene was finished. Melissa's mom reattached it when he returned backstage.

When it was time for their musical number, Sophie forgot her terror; the four girls sang out clearly and in perfect harmony. For the closing scene, the whole cast joined in the final chorus:

Someday we'll build a school in this wonderful town,
In this beautiful valley of ours.
A school where children go,
To be taught what they should know
Someday, in this valley of ours.

After the performance, everyone streamed into the gymnasium, which was decorated with balloons and posters. The walls were lined with tables loaded with platters of sandwiches and sweets. Felicia chose egg salad with no crusts and a round spiral of bread and creamy salmon with a pickle in the middle.

"There you are!" Delia wanted to take another picture. "Say cheese."

"My mouth's full."

"Swallow and smile."

"Where's my little niece? All grown up, star of stage and screen!" Felicia felt herself enveloped in her Aunt Vi's warm embrace, up against cushiony breasts. Beyond her aunt stood a grinning Lenore and Rosalee, waiting for their turn to hug Felicia.

"There's lots to eat, yummy sandwiches and cookies," said Felicia, stepping back and adjusting the bonnet that was still tied around her chin.

"Get rid of that headgear," said Rosalee.

"You look amazingly strange with all that makeup," said Lenore.

"I know."

"Like a different person."

"I'm still me. Have a sandwich."

Conversation was difficult in the crush and confusion of so many people. Felicia managed to introduce Rosalee and Lenore to Renate and Sophie. Dodie was too far away, across the gym.

Mr. Butler appeared in their midst, red-faced and beaming. He said to Florence, "You must be so proud of your talented daughter."

"Yes, I am, but Felicia is my granddaughter. Let me introduce you to my daughters, Delia and Vivian." The drama teacher made a courtly bow.

Felicia eased her mother and family away from the smarmy Mr. Butler and whispered, "Can we go home?"

"Sure we can, what's the matter?"

"I don't think Lenore and Rosalee are having any fun."

CHAPTER 51
Flower

THE WOMAN'S EYES brightened with interest as they focused on Flower. "Here's a hardy young girl. She'll be helpful to us."

Eldon nodded his head in agreement. He said, "She surely has been helpful, tending us when we were sick and making her way alone to the Buxtons'."

"That so?"

Flower started to describe their experiences, but the people in the house were saying hello and pulling out chairs.

Gabriel was lifted out of his sling. "Oh! A fine baby!" He received a loud kiss on each cheek.

They settled around the table and Eldon recounted the details of their journey. Hazel nodded. "Now it's time for the last leg."

"How far have we got to go?"

"We'll head for Erie. Then you'll be in Pennsylvania."

"Will we be safe there?" Flower asked.

"Someone like you, with bounty hunters at your heels,

there's only one safe place, and that's out of the country. Once we're in Erie, we'll cross the lake to Canada, where you'll be free within the law. You can stay with me for a while in a town called St. Catharines; then I'll find you a place where you can be useful till spring."

"Thank you. We are so grateful for your help."

"This is what I do. I'm glad to do it."

"Do you have a map we can look at?"

"It's all in my head."

Flower noticed her father's doubtful glance. "All in your head?"

"She's done it many a time," said Abe. "You're in good hands."

Hazel said, "I've helped many people. Haven't lost one yet."

They left the next morning, once more bidding farewell to kind strangers. They spent three days traveling on foot through fields and forests, and by road, hidden in wagons. The first night they slept in a haystack in a barnyard, and the second night they slept among the gravestones in a churchyard. At the last station, they were again hidden in an attic.

Flower bedded down on a straw-filled mattress next to Hazel. She glanced at the woman beside her and stretched out her legs, comparing their length to Hazel's. "You're just a little bit bigger than me."

"That's right."

"Your hair is getting gray, so you're not going to grow any taller."

Hazel's laugh was husky and dry, as if it was rarely used. "I'm tall enough. Time to settle and get some rest. We have a big day tomorrow."

"Lots more walking?"

"No. Tomorrow we take a boat."

Flower was instantly wary. "I don't like boats. I know they can sink, and I can't swim."

"Don't worry. This one is safe. It's made many a trip. Now that's enough talk. Time for sleep." Hazel rolled over on her side, with her back to Flower, signaling the end of their conversation.

The next morning the family was given new clothes to wear. Flower was outfitted with trousers and cap.

Cleo looked at her daughter with surprise. "You look just like a boy! Is that what Gabriel is going to be like?"

Eldon was also given dark clothing and cap, and Cleo was given a new dress and wide-brimmed bonnet. "There," said Hazel. "Keep the babe hidden as much as you can with your cloak. Try to look like a different family, more prosperous, as if you know where you are going and have every right to be doing it."

The group stood nervously on the pier the next

morning—Flower slightly apart from her family and closer to Hazel, who was also dressed in long pants like a man. The lake glistened before them, stretching endlessly to the horizon.

"Here, boy. Carry this case for me." With his foot, a stranger shoved a suitcase in Flower's direction. She hesitated, uncertain. "And hurry up about it." Flower carried the case to a footbridge leading up to the boat. "Here you go," the man said, flipping a coin. It landed and glistened in the dirt. She retrieved it and ran back to Hazel.

"Come stand beside me. Let's wait behind these bales. When most people are on board, someone will come out and get us."

"Who?"

"Mr. Brown. He's a colored man who's done well. He owns three ships that sail these lakes. His gift to us is free passage."

Flower looked with wonder at the lake, waves lapping against the immense vessel that towered over her. There were gold letters outlined in black on its side.

M-O-R-N-I-N-G S-T-A-R

"Do you know what that says, Hazel?"

"No. I can't read. I wish I knew how. The first thing you should do when you get free and settled is learn to read. It's a wonderful thing."

"I would really like to."

Once aboard, Flower was ushered down below with Hazel, away from her family. She tried to be invisible as she stared at the plank floor and listened to the rough thrum of the boat tracking across the water. After a while, Hazel led her up to the deck, and together they stood against the railing. Flower felt the wind fly against her face as the boat sliced through waves, closer and closer to the shore.

There was a shocking blast of a horn just before docking. Thick ropes were tossed down and tied to posts. The passengers massed into a crowd, waved to those waiting for them, and then shuffled in orderly rows down to the pier. Flower could see her mother and father ahead, already on land. She felt like pushing others aside and running down to join them, but she stayed quietly in line. When her feet left the swaying boat and touched solid ground, she raced toward her mother's open arms. Hazel followed close behind and joined the family. They came together into a circle, not saying a word, arms extended around each other in a mutual and grateful embrace.

CHAPTER 52
Felicia

AT HOME, Felicia headed straight for the shower, then reappeared cleansed of stage makeup and more comfortably dressed in jeans and sweatshirt. She found her friends watching television. "Who's up for some popcorn?"

Lenore had Rufus in her lap and was stroking his purring head. She glanced up at Felicia and said, "You look better now."

"I feel better too."

Florence called out from the kitchen. "There's chili in the slow cooker and bread on the counter. You girls come and help yourselves to a meal."

They came into the kitchen. Delia was tossing salad, Aunt Vi slicing bread. They filled their bowls and sat around the table, talking and laughing together.

"That was quite the production, Felicia," said Aunt Vi.

"Mr. Butler did a fine job," said Delia. "He introduced himself to us in the gym."

"I don't like him," said Felicia.

"You don't? Why not?" asked her mother.

Felicia didn't want to tarnish the jolly mood, but Delia looked steadily at her until she answered. "He didn't want me to be a pioneer...He wanted me to be a 'Native' instead. But I protested, so he finally agreed."

Delia's expression hardened, but her voice was calm. "I'm going to have a conversation with him about that."

"Mom."

"Don't worry about it. Sometimes even teachers need teaching."

"Oh, that man's going to get a lesson." Aunt Vi chuckled and shook her head.

Delia went to the front room to turn off the television and put on some music. She sang along as the table was cleared. After the cleanup, Aunt Vi dealt the cards at he women sat down to play.

Lenore looked on and suggested, "Why don't you play your queen of diamonds?"

"Don't go giving my hand away now, this is serious stuff!"

Felicia stood behind her mother's chair and began to braid her hair. "Remember I used to brush your hair when you played cards?"

"I do. It felt grand. But you can forget the hair and make us some fudge."

The girls made two plates. They left one with the women

in the kitchen and took the other upstairs. Lenore brought Rufus, who stretched out on the bed like one of the group.

"It was weird being at your school," Lenore said. "So many white faces. Is it hard living here?"

"It is, sometimes," said Felicia. "Some people can be really mean. And stupid. But Dodie and Renate and Sophie are nice. They got me into riding. I have a horse named Morning Star. Well, I don't own her—she belongs to my riding teacher—but she's the only one I ride. She's so beautiful. Maybe tomorrow before you leave, I can take you to see her at the stables?"

"Wow, a horse!" said Rosalee. "I can't picture it, but I guess that's pretty cool."

Laughter from the kitchen drifted upstairs, but Lenore's face was solemn. "Felicia, have you changed?"

"No. I'm still the same person. I'm just doing some new things."

"Meeting new people," said Rosalee.

"Yes."

"Making new friends."

"I am. But I don't want to lose my old friends, like you two. You are my oldest and best friends."

"Really?"

"Yes, really. Honestly."

Rufus lifted his left rear leg and began to lick the rounded pads of his paw, his back curved into a perfect arch.

263

"Okay, but what about us? How can we be friends if you have this new life in a different town?"

"We can talk—Mom says we can get hooked up to the Internet soon, so that we'll make it easier. And you guys can come and see me, and I'll come and see you. You said I could come down and visit you. Didn't you mean it?"

"Yes, but do you still want to?"

"Of course I'm coming! I'm going to come down and pound on your door till you let me in. I'll make so much noise the neighbors will be yelling at you. You'll have to let me in." Felicia tapped Lenore on the top of her head with a pillow. Lenore picked up another pillow, and Rosalee threw a sock. Rufus watched the giggling bedlam with interest, then yawned and stretched, fanning all his toes and extending all his toenails before settling on his side.

CHAPTER 53
Flower

FLOWER LUGGED a heavy rock to the growing pile under the tree. Gabriel toddled after her, his hands full of stones. He threw them at the collection. "See Flower?"

"Yes, I see what a helpful boy you are. Come and get some more."

Her father and two other men worked steadily, choosing each stone according to its size and shape, setting it in with the others, crafting a fence that would last for generations.

"This ground's been growing nothing but rocks."

"Since the beginning of time."

"Next year this field will be golden with grain."

"I can taste it now."

Flower brought them one more stone, then looked down at her hands, scraped and sore.

"Pa, my hands are done with carrying for now."

"Fetch us a pitcher of something cold and tasty then."

Flower took Gabriel's reluctant hand and led him back to their house. His howling "no!" could be heard all the way to the front yard.

Cleo appeared in the doorway. "What's all the noise about?"

"Gabriel wants to stay and help Pa, but he's just in the way without me to tend him. My hands are sore and Pa's thirsty."

Cleo opened her arms to her disgruntled little boy. "We'll make up some cold tea."

Flower carried a pail to the pump. She worked the handle up and down to get the water flowing, rinsed out the pail and set it aside, then thrust her scratched palms under the cascading water, enjoying the icy relief.

She heard someone whistling over the sound of the running water. Flower looked back to where her father was working and then up at the road. A man walked along with his hands in his pockets, a bag slung over his shoulder. Flower squinted into the distance. There was something familiar about him. He came closer, and she recognized him.

"Samuel!" Flower stopped pumping water and rushed back to the house. "Ma! It's Samuel coming down the road!" She turned from the door and ran toward the field. "Pa! Come quick and see who's here!"

Her father dropped a stone and trotted to the front of

the house. Cleo came to the doorway. "Welcome! Welcome! You're a sight for sore eyes!"

"Isn't he, though? How did you know where to find us?"

"I heard about you, and I thought to myself how I'd like to see you folks again!"

Eldon made introductions to the neighbors. "This is our friend who we met on our journey."

"Seems like a lifetime ago," said Samuel.

"Not so long, just two years."

"How've you been? Come in and we'll have a meal, all of us. We were just making some tea."

They settled around the table. "So, tell us where you've been and how you've been doing," said Eldon.

"It's been a mighty long road. Thought I'd never be warm and dry again. Once, I even spent a whole day hiding up to my neck in a pond amongst the reeds."

"Just like Moses."

"He, at least, was in a basket." As they laughed, Samuel turned his gaze to Gabriel. "Look at that boy, a baby no longer." His eyes found Flower. "And your daughter, growing into a beautiful young lady."

Flower searched out her mother's reassuring face. "I forgot the pail of water. I'll go get it."

Samuel stood up. "I'll help you."

They walked across the yard to the pump. "Tell me

how you've been, Flower. Was it a hard journey for you to come here?"

"Yes."

"I always tried to picture you and your family safe from harm."

"We were caught. Papa was treated real bad. They put us in a jail." Flower's voice trembled with the retelling. Samuel took her hand, but she withdrew it and started to pump water into the pail.

"I never was caught, but I sure got hungry. I know eggs taste better cooked."

There was a bench near the pump. They sat down together. Flower said, "You cooked squirrels for us."

"You remember that?"

"Yes." Flower studied her lap, then looked up at the side of Samuel's head. "Your wound has healed nicely." Her finger traced the fluted remnant of an ear. "Does it pain you at all?"

"Just on a windy day."

They sat and gazed at the bay, glistening blue in the distance.

"A man could die of thirst waiting for you two!" Eldon shouted from the house. "And it's time for lunch."

As they ate their bread and cheese, Samuel asked, "What about you folk? You're looking fine."

"After we crossed the water, we stayed with some people for a while, waiting for Cleo to recover her strength," said Eldon. "I helped and worked on their farm, made enough money to buy a horse and wagon. We came up here a while back. What you see is what we have."

"You own some land?"

"That I do."

"My dream," said Samuel.

"Stay here. This is a good community. We help each other."

Cleo stood and wiped her hands on her apron. "Eldon, it's time for the Women's Institute meeting. Flower and I are on our way. Gabriel will be in your care, on his best behavior." She gave an emphatic look to her little boy.

Flower took her mother's arm as they left the house. "Feeling all right?"

Cleo arched her back, took slow steps. "I'm thinking our wee visitor can make its presence known anytime."

Flower glanced at her mother's swollen belly. She couldn't imagine the arrival of this 'visitor' would be an easy process. The neighboring women had promised to help when the time came, especially Mrs. Perkins, who was said to be proficient in handling such matters.

When they arrived at the community hall, a neighbor took Cleo's other arm. "Here's the healthy mother and her daughter. We're all set."

They joined four other women grouped around a quilt stretched and held in place by a wooden frame. Flower settled her mother comfortably in a chair, then sat down herself and picked up a needle. Her hands were sore from gathering stones and, in spite of a season of quilting, the needle still felt awkward in her fingers; but she enjoyed listening to the women talk as they created a work of art that would keep someone warm on a cold winter night.

"Hear you folks have a visitor."

"Someone we met when we started our journey. We had to travel different paths because he was recovering from a wound. Now he's fine."

"Is he staying?"

"Might be—for a while."

"We'll have a meeting, hear him speak."

"Good idea."

"Flower, how you doing there?" Mrs. Perkins glanced across the expanse of colored fabric.

"My stitches are still crooked."

"Improving all the time."

"Do we sign this?"

"Sign it! How are we going to do that?" The women laughed together.

"I was thinking of embroidering a flower in the corner here, where I've been working."

"I think that's a fine idea. Here, start with some yellow for the center." Mrs. Perkins bit through the extended thread with her teeth, then licked one end before aiming it through the eye of the needle. "Watch how I'm doing this." She plunged the needle into the fabric. "This is called a French knot."

"Thank you." Flower studied the twisting and stitching and then tried it herself. "Ma, do you recall Hettie?"

Cleo lifted her head. "Yes, I do, the Jensons—all those children."

"Hettie gave me a flower when we left. She asked me to keep it and think of her."

"Do you still have it?"

"No, but I do remember her." Flower pushed and pulled the thread through the layers of cotton, crosshatching colors, creating delicate flower petals. "I wonder if she remembers me."

No one answered. There was a companionable silence as the women bent over their work. Within her own thoughts, Flower decided that Hettie would remember her, would sometimes think of her and wish her well. As she sewed, faces and voices from the past paraded through her mind: the Pembertons, kind Sarah and heroic Noah, Dr. Simon, Jake, Abe and Abigail Buxton, odd-looking and brave little Hazel. Then the vivid memories of the near drowning, escaping from jail, and the fury of the mob. She stopped stitching.

"What is it, Flower?"

"Just resting." It was good to be in a safe place.

CHAPTER 54
Felicia

FELICIA PEERED through the microscope. The tiny flatworm's severed tail had started to grow back.

"Awesome! Have a look, Sophie." Felicia vacated her position next to the instrument and wrote her observations in a notebook.

"Oh, thank goodness, it's going to be all right."

Renate had a turn. "It's looking back at us!"

"Maybe it should have a name," suggested Sophie.

"Puleeeze!" Dodie rolled her eyes. "It's a worm!"

"It's a living creature. We should treat it with respect."

"That doesn't mean we treat it like a pet. We cut it in half!"

Their teacher joined their group. "How are you doing?"

"Our worm's growing where we cut him."

Miss Peabody had a quick look through the eye-piece. "Don't forget to note your observations. Five more minutes."

The students returned to their work as the teacher strolled among them, glancing at notebooks, adjusting magnification, and making suggestions. She asked the class, "What are your thoughts on this creature?"

"That it's ugly and disgusting."

"Ashley, that statement seems harsh and without reflection. I'm sure you can do better than that."

"It's true."

"Anyone else? Yes, Josh."

"It's neat that it can renew itself. It would be good if we could figure out how it does that."

"Why would that be good?"

"'Cause then maybe we could grow parts of ourselves if we needed them."

"Can you think of examples?"

Felicia remembered an uncle of Lenore's who had burned his hand in an accident. The scars restricted the movement of his fingers. She said, "People who've had bad burns—it would be good if they could grow new skin."

"Or grow new white skin." Ashley's stage whisper created a hush in the classroom.

"I beg your pardon!" Miss Peabody's head pivoted like that of a barn owl suddenly aware of a mouse. "What did you just say?"

Felicia braced herself for a repeat of the nasty phrase, but Ashley was silent.

"I think you owe the class an apology," Miss Peabody persisted.

"Sorry." Ashley's voice could barely be heard.

In the quiet that followed, Felicia was grateful that the teacher had not asked Ashley to apologize directly to her.

At the end of class, Miss Peabody announced, "Enjoy your lunch. I'd like to see you all in front of the school at 1:15. There will be a bus waiting to take us to the Sheffield Park Black History and Culture Museum." In a much quieter voice, she added, "Ashley, will you stay behind for a moment? I'd like to have a word with you."

This was the first field trip of the school year, so the bus ride was predictably lively. The driver made them stay in their seats, but couldn't quell the din of twenty-five voices or the flight of paper missiles. Miss Peabody sat at the front and read a book, trying to ignore the chaos.

When they arrived at their destination, the students tumbled out of the coziness of the bus into chilled sunlight, so bright it made them blink. The recent snowfall had disappeared, but there was a hint in the November air of more to come. Forming random groups, they made their way from the corner of the highway down to the bay. Felicia admired the colors of the water, green deepening to blue farther out, whitecaps fringing waves as they furled into shore. Overhead, strings of late-departing geese angled into formation, calling to each other.

The museum was at the base of the street, where the beach met the water. Remnants of fishing skiffs lay embedded in the sand, like the bony carcasses of ancient animals. The faded gray-frame building was nestled among the broken boats.

The curator stood at the door, her eyes lively behind large frames. "Welcome, everyone! I'm Mrs. Wilson. Are you frozen? You must be. Come in and get warm. I've made you some hot apple cider, just the thing for a day like today. Winter's on its way, don't you think?" They were directed from coat hooks to a table set with plates of cookies. Mrs. Wilson ladled the steaming cider into mugs.

Felicia sipped the fragrant liquid as she moved from the treat table toward the historical artifacts. There were horse collars and lace collars, plow blades and buttoned boots, photographs and faded letters, and, side by side on one wall, a spinning wheel and a pump organ.

Josh ran his fingers across the keys. "What did people do for fun a long time ago?"

"They listened to music, often making their own. They helped each other, especially in small communities such as ours. If someone needed a barn, all the men would get together and build one. The women organized quilting bees. And now that leads me to show you something special."

She led them into another room and stood in front of a colorful embroidered quilt. "This is like an artist's canvas, only made with cloth, not paint. A very talented woman created it and donated it to the museum. It shows the geography and routes of the Underground Railroad." She began to tell the story. "In the early part of the nineteenth century, escaped slaves made the difficult journey from the southern United States north, to freedom. Our community was one of their destinations.

"There was no train, of course. Most people walked, or traveled hidden in wagons, or came in boats down rivers and across lakes. The term 'underground' meant it was a secret." As she spoke, Mrs. Wilson used her finger to trace a route depicted, stitch by stitch, over mountains, up rivers. "They followed the North Star and, if they traveled in the spring, the geese flying north. You can see how these things have been included in the design of the quilt."

"What did they do when they got here?"

"Settled in. They farmed, started businesses, and built schools, just like any other newcomer. And they're part of our history here."

Felicia stared at the quilt. Here was the history she had been reading about. She imagined what it must have been like to escape, to travel such long distances, hoping for a final safe haven. "They were so brave."

"Yes, they were brave."

Miss Peabody continued the tour with most of the class trailing behind her. Felicia stood back, absorbed with the quilt. Renate joined her. "Isn't that amazing? All that work."

"Yeah, it is."

"There's another one in the corner, not as nice. It's raggedy and old."

The two girls crossed the room. Renate stopped to look at a fan displayed in a glass case while Felicia studied the second quilt. The traditional patchwork pattern was worn and faded, but it had a dignified charm. She stepped closer, her eyes wandering over the appliquéd fabric, following the tiny white stitches. There was something different about the bottom corner. Felicia felt herself drawn to it, but knew she shouldn't touch it. Glancing over her shoulder, she saw the curator deep in conversation with Miss Peabody, not paying attention.

Felicia reached out with the tips of her fingers and traced the soft embroidered cotton, small, round knots of thread in the center, fragments of cloth shaped like petals, faded and fraying, but unmistakably a flower.

Acknowledgments

A few years ago I discovered that I lived in a place where slaves from the southern United States had made their way to freedom in what once was a terminus of the Underground Railroad. This history inspired me, and I decided to write a story for young people. I visited the Black History Museum, located now in Clarksburg, Ontario, and met Carolyn Wilson. She was busy doing some maintenance work but put down her paintbrush, and we talked as she proudly showed me the exhibits in different buildings.

Seeking information, I read several books. One was the biography of Josiah Henson, a man born into slavery in 1789. He eventually became a conductor for the Underground Railroad, helped found a community for escaped slaves in Canada, and traveled widely, speaking out against slavery. In his biography, he related the story of his father's abuse at the hands of a slave owner. As punishment for his attempted escape, Henson's father's ear was severed. This image stayed in my mind and I used it to describe the fate of one of my characters.

When my book was near completion I decided to take a course of study in creative writing at Humber College. I submitted this novel and worked with Lawrence Hill, award-winning author of *The Book of Negroes* (published as *Someone Knows My Name* in the United States, Australia, and New Zealand). His suggestions were thoughtful and insightful, and I enjoyed his mentorship immensely.

I am grateful that Second Story Press's Margie Wolfe and Carolyn Jackson took a chance on an unknown writer, providing me with constructive suggestions and encouragement. Alison Kooistra's perceptive and skillful editing was invaluable in shaping the final manuscript.

Family is often the backbone that provides the support for any extended endeavor, and mine is no exception. My love and thanks to them, especially my husband Leonard, whose computer skills and good humor were always readily and generously available.

About the Author

JUDITH PLAXTON is a retired nurse with an avid interest in the environment, local history, and volunteering: she fund raises for the Stephen Lewis Foundation, is involved with the Georgian Lifelong Learning Institute, and visits her local elementary school to help children in the language department. She lives in Clarksburg, Ontario, a small community on the Niagara Escarpment.